Deborah

Also by James R. Shott
in Large Print:

Hagar
Joseph
Leah

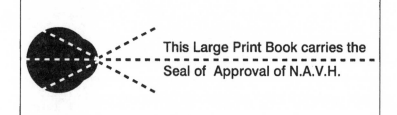

This Large Print Book carries the
Seal of Approval of N.A.V.H.

Deborah

JAMES R. SHOTT

Thorndike Press • Waterville, Maine

Published in 2001 by arrangement with Herald Press, a division of Mennonite Publishing House, Inc.

Thorndike Press Large Print Christian Fiction Series.

The tree indicium is a trademark of Thorndike Press.

The text of this Large Print edition is unabridged.
Other aspects of the book may vary from the original edition.

Set in 16 pt. Plantin by Christina S. Huff.

Printed in the United States on permanent paper.

Library of Congress Cataloging-in-Publication Data

Shott, James R., 1925–
    Deborah / James R. Shott.
        p.   cm.
    ISBN 0-7862-3593-4 (lg. print : hc : alk. paper)
    1. Deborah (Biblical judge) — Fiction.   2. Bible. O.T. — History of Biblical events — Fiction.   3. Women in the Bible — Fiction.   4. Large type books.   I. Title.
PS3569.H598 D4 2001
    813'.54—dc21   2001041562

*To Dana, Carrie, and Lara Shane,
granddaughters, whose enthusiasm,
vitality, and obvious enjoyment
of life keep me young.*

1

I grasped my half-brother's arm. "Look, Rakem," I said. "Someone's coming."

"Where, Beriah?" he asked.

"There."

His eyes followed my pointing finger across the valley, where the rugged road north to Shechem topped the hill. Pine trees almost obscured the far side of the valley. A gnarled oak tree, blasted by lightning a few years before, contrasted with the stately pines. The trail wound around moss-covered rocks, with purple thistle blooms adding a spark of color in the early dry season.

Through the trees we could see, in the distance, a lone runner descending the slope toward us. Running fast.

"It's Modan," Rakem said.

I nodded. Rakem's son Modan was the fastest youth in our squad of warriors. That was why he had been sent ahead as a scout.

Rakem ruffled his gray-streaked beard. "Trouble," he muttered.

"Yes." I had guessed from the moment I spotted the youth that someone on the other side of that hill was coming toward us. Someone who was a threat to our small contingent of twelve warriors. Since leaving Bethel early this morning, we had as yet met no one on the road.

We watched in silence as the youth reached the bottom of the valley and began the steep climb up the road toward where we waited. We could see him clearly now, his short skirt held high as he ran. Sweat glistened on his forehead in the noonday sun. He carried no spear; his job was to warn us of trouble, not to fight an enemy.

Modan came to a stop ten feet from us, his chest heaving. "Someone's . . . coming!" he gasped. "On the road . . . on the other side . . . of that hill!"

"How many?" barked Rakem.

"Twenty-eight men." Modan sucked air into his lungs. "With spears and swords!"

Armed men. Trouble. I frowned. "Canaanites?"

"I don't know," replied Modan. "But they wear bronze helmets."

"Who wears bronze armor in this part of the country?" I wondered out loud.

"Kenites, most likely." Rakem again ran his fingers through his beard. "If so, I hope they're friendly. But you never know with Kenites. We'd better be ready."

Kenites! The ancient tribe of metalsmiths had become increasingly warlike in recent years, forsaking their forges to roam around the country plundering. Mostly they raided Canaanite villages, leaving the Israelites alone. They had learned to respect us, from hard experience. But Rakem was right; you never knew about Kenites.

The band of armed men topped the hill across the valley and came jogging down the slope. Yes, they were Kenites; I could see their bronze breastplates. Each man carried a spear and sword. Modan had been right — I counted twenty-eight, more than a match for our dozen.

"This is as good a place as any to defend," said Rakem. "You men, hobble the donkey. Form a circle around this knoll, drawn tight, with your spears —"

"Wait, Rakem." I placed my hand on his arm. "Let's not fight." I turned to my men. "Lay down your spears," I said, "and raise your right hands in greeting."

"No, Beriah!" Rakem gripped his spear tightly. "Let's at least go down fighting, like Israelites!"

Rakem was seventeen years older than I, the fighting man of the family. His knowledge of diplomacy extended no farther than his spearpoint.

"Put it down, brother," I said firmly. "There will be no fighting today."

"But —"

"Put it down!"

He glared at me for a moment, but in the end he dropped his spear on the ground.

"Now raise your hand," I said.

Rakem muttered something unintelligible, but slowly raised his hand like the rest of us, in the universal sign of friendship.

The Kenites were now jogging up the hill, near enough for us to see their faces. Their leader was a powerfully built man, his gray hair stringy, long, and dripping with sweat and grime. He looked old, about forty.

Rakem grunted. "I know him. Heber. He's wild."

I had heard of Heber the Kenite. He came from the country around the Sea of Chinnereth. His reputation for ferocity was legendary.

"What's he doing this far south?" I asked.

"Raiding. Yahweh damn him!"

"Rakem!"

"Sorry, brother."

I knew Rakem must be upset, to utter a blasphemy in my presence. He knew how I felt about that. This was not the time, how-

10

ever, to lecture him about taking God's name in vain.

The Kenites, at a word from their leader, spread out and surrounded us, their spears menacing. They eyed the packs on our donkey greedily.

I smiled. "Greetings to Heber the Kenite. May Yahweh give you good fortune. We come in friendship."

Heber's barrel chest heaved a few times as he tried to control his breathing. When he spoke, his voice was deep and guttural.

"Who are you, and where are you going?"

"I am Beriah *ben* Jonathan of the tribe of Ephraim. I live in Bethel, and I am going to Shechem to claim my bride."

The big Kenite snorted. "I've heard of you. You're the poet. Hah! The *empty* poet." The emphasis on the word accompanied a sneer.

The term was ambiguous. It could be derogatory, referring to the substance of my poetry, empty of meaning and intelligence. Or it could mean simply that it was bare poetry, devoid of music. I chose to believe the latter; I could neither sing nor play an instrument. My poetry *was* empty.

Rakem, however, chose to interpret his words as an insult. "Kenite dog," he muttered.

Heber swung around and stared at Rakem, his red cheeks growing darker. "Who are you?" he demanded.

I spoke hastily. "Please forgive my brother's hasty words."

"Brother?" He glared at Rakem. "You must be that snotty Rakem. I remember you."

"And I remember you, Kenite dog! I offered to fight you once. I'll do it now, if your bowels don't turn to water."

"Pick up your spear, then!"

"No!" I stepped between them, facing Rakem. "We come in peace, Heber. There will be no fighting among us. You hear me, Rakem?"

"C'mon, Beriah —"

"No fighting!" I ordered.

My face was close to his, and his burning eyes met mine. He knew I meant it. I was only twenty-one, seventeen years younger than he, but he always deferred to me. I liked to think it was because he respected my judgment, not just that I was the rightful heir, the only legitimate son of Jonathan.

Abruptly Rakem turned and strode back a few steps to stand with our men. I breathed easier.

Turning to the Kenite, I said, "This is not a day for fighting. It's my wedding week."

Heber's eyes softened. "All right. No

brawling on your wedding journey. Shechem, you say? You going to marry one of those wenches from Manasseh?"

"No, my friend. I go to marry the daughter of a son of Ephraim."

He frowned. "There are only two Ephraimites at Shechem. Becher's daughter is already married. And Tahan's daughters are fat. You want a fat wife?"

"No, Heber. I will marry Becher's other daughter. And she's not fat."

He snorted. "I didn't know he had another one."

"She's young."

"The best kind. Hah? Train 'em right. Be sure you beat her now and then."

I didn't want this discussion to go any further. "Why don't you come visit us at Bethel? When we celebrate the weaning of our first son."

The old man grinned, showing gaps between his teeth. "Yeah. I will. I'll bring my wife Jael, and our three sons. When? In four years?"

"Three, if Yahweh is kind."

He laughed. "Yahweh doesn't do it all, boy. You gotta do something too."

I raised my hand, hoping he would interpret it as a farewell gesture. "Yahweh bless you, my friend."

He chose to ignore my signals. "Do you know," Heber said slowly, "I think we'll go to Shechem with you. We'll join in the wedding celebration at Becher's house. Hah! They'll have good wine and lots of meat. What say, men?"

The Kenites grinned and grunted words of agreement. I frowned. These wild men at Shechem . . . who knew what would happen?

He noticed my frown. "Don't worry, bridegroom. We won't cause any trouble. I respect the laws of hospitality. Do you think we're Canaanites?"

"No . . . it's just that . . . well, they're only expecting twelve guests. We'll have to let them know."

"All right then. I'll send one of my men to tell them."

"Er, Heber, it might be better if I send one of my men. Yes. I'll send Rakem."

He grinned. "You're a sly one, poet. Sending Rakem. To make sure we don't fight, eh?"

I grinned back. "That's wise, isn't it?"

He threw back his head and guffawed. "By Hobab, you're smart, boy. All right, send that pig brother of yours. Then I won't be tempted to break the laws of hospitality *and* a few of his bones."

Rakem, who was standing only a few feet

away, heard all of this. His face turned red under his black and gray beard. He glanced longingly at his spear, which was still on the ground.

"Rakem, come here." I picked up his spear and walked away from Heber to talk to Rakem. Then I spoke softly.

"Tell Becher they're coming. And please, brother, tomorrow at the wedding feast, don't pick a fight with Heber!"

"What if he calls me a pig again?" To call an Israelite a pig was just as insulting as calling a Kenite a dog.

"I'll talk to him. He seems to respect the laws of hospitality."

Rakem spat. "If you can trust him."

I looked sharply at Rakem. "What happened between you two?" I asked.

"Twenty years ago, he was a guest in our house. We almost fought then. But father wouldn't permit it."

"Why did he come to your house?"

Rakem shrugged. "Supplies. A meal. Your mother was pregnant with you at the time. Father was very nervous until he left."

I nodded, picturing the scene. Rakem, a brash sixteen year old, must have sneered at the barbaric visitor, who would have responded fiercely. Father's wise intervention had probably prevented a lot of bloodshed, including my own while still in my mother's womb.

My birth was important to our father Jonathan. His first wife was barren. Following the custom established in the time of Abraham, he had taken her handmaid, a Canaanite slave to his bed. She had given him one son — Rakem.

But when Father married a second wife and I was born, Rakem was instantly disinherited. Instead of resenting me, he had become my companion, guardian, and first lieutenant. After Father's death a year ago, I took over the management of his estates. Rakem could never have handled the problems and intricacies of this large an establishment. Flocks and herds, gardens, servants, three separate estates — it was certainly a challenge. I had little time for my poetry.

"Go to Shechem as fast as you can," I handed Rakem his spear. "You should be there before sundown. We'll probably be there later tonight."

He nodded and left, jogging down the trail to the north. I watched him climb the rise and disappear over the hill. Then I turned back to Heber, and with the Kenites we resumed our uneasy journey north.

Heber walked beside me. Old he may have been, but he walked with an easy lope and never seemed to tire. I hoped he would be too concerned with keeping up with me to have breath left to talk, but I hoped in vain.

"How long have you been betrothed to the daughter of Becher?" he asked bluntly.

I resigned myself to answering his personal questions. What else could I do? We were now traveling companions and presumably friends.

"Eleven years."

He whistled through his uneven teeth. "Eleven years! She must have been a baby."

"She was three. I was ten."

"She ready now?"

I took a deep breath. These questions were becoming more personal. I knew what he meant. Just two months ago, a messenger had arrived from Becher saying his daughter Deborah had arrived at puberty and was now ready for marriage.

"Yes," I replied tersely.

He glanced at me. Maybe I had communicated to him some of my uneasiness with his questions of so personal a nature. But that didn't seem to deter him.

"That Rakem brother of yours. He married?"

I knew why he was asking. No younger son should marry before the heir to the estate. So I answered his unspoken implica-

17

tion. "Yes, but Rakem is not our father Jonathan's heir. I am."

"Yeah? How did you manage that?"

And that's how our discussion went that afternoon, as we trudged the long miles toward Shechem. I patiently explained to him our family history, careful always to be polite. He seemed interested. We paused at a brook to refresh ourselves. I divided with Heber my dried goat meat and barley cakes, while he shared with me a skin of good wine which he carried on his shoulder. I wondered what unfortunate Canaanite household he had raided to steal their wine.

I said, "My friend, what do you plan to wear for a wedding garment?"

He grinned. "What I have on now. Does it matter?"

It mattered to most cultured Israelites, but obviously not to him. Guests who did not wear a formal robe at a wedding were considered rude. His ragged, dirty burnoose over armor would be out of place in a formal wedding.

He noticed my hesitation. "You have an extra wedding garment you could lend me?"

"No. I brought only one. It wouldn't fit you anyway."

He glanced over at the donkey with its laden pack, then turned back to me. "Let me see," he said brusquely.

Why did he want to see it? Would he try to take it from me forceably? Improbable. One who respected the laws of hospitality would not insult his traveling companion.

I opened one of the packs on the donkey's back and pulled out my carefully folded garment. It was new and white with purple sash and trim. I held it up for him to see that it would be much too small for him.

"Purple!" Heber seemed genuinely impressed.

Purple was an extremely expensive color to have in a robe. It came from Phoenicia, where the dye was made from sea creatures by a secret formula. I would look elegant tomorrow at the nuptial ceremony.

Heber frowned. "Maybe I could borrow a wedding garment from Becher."

"Maybe. He's a big man. And rich. He'll have extras." He nodded then glanced at the sun, now sinking toward the western horizon.

We resumed the journey of the last few miles to Shechem. Heber seemed eager to renew his discussion with me. This time, however, I steered the conversation away from my personal life and onto his.

"Tell me, Heber. Do you still mine copper and forge tools?"

The Kenites had been known for centuries as metalsmiths. They also claimed to be descendants of Jethro, Moses' father-in-law, although our tradition tells us Jethro was a Midianite, not a Kenite. A few families had come with Moses at the time of the exodus from Egypt. They had never mixed their blood with ours, even though we believed in the same God. They were not as careful about keeping the law of Moses.

"We do," he said in reply to my question. "We make mostly arms now. See this breastplate? This helmet? This sword? Spearpoint? I made them myself. Good workmanship. We use them more than garden tools."

I knew what he meant. The Kenites were infamous throughout Israel for raiding and plundering the Canaanites. Sometimes they even attacked Israelites.

"And what of your family, Heber? Many sons?"

He nodded. "Three. All grown and married. My wife Jael lives near Kedesh. Come visit us sometime. Jael loves to have guests. Once she even entertained the king of Hazor."

The king of Hazor! That would be Jabin, one of the most powerful of all the Canaanite kings.

"You aren't taking up with the Canaanites, are you?" I asked.

He laughed. "Only the rich and powerful. The others I raid. Most of my friends are Israelites. Like Barak."

"Barak?"

"Yeah. The son of Abinoam, tribe of Naphtali. He lives in Kedesh. Good man, Barak. Has a small army, and a lot more like us he can count on when trouble comes. If it weren't for him, King Jabin would be making big trouble for all you Israelites."

I listened to Heber prate on and on. Darkness came as we walked, but the moon and stars were all the light we needed. The road was broad. I was glad when we finally arrived at Shechem. Maybe tomorrow Heber would transfer his need to talk to our host, Becher, my future father-in-law.

As we approached Becher's manor house, my mind wandered from Heber's endless chatter and contemplated my future. By tomorrow I would be married. What would that be like? What new experiences awaited me with a woman companion? I hoped she would be a good wife. Her father was a true son of Israel. Surely he had instilled in her the traditions of marriage and family which our people hold dear. I determined to talk to her about that.

The only time I had met Deborah was eleven years ago, when our fathers had celebrated our betrothal. I recall her as an awkward three-year-old, a little thin, not very pretty. My father Jonathan had been pleased with this betrothal. The union of two important Ephraimite families would ensure a prosperous future.

Becher, Deborah's father, was probably the wealthiest man in all Ephraim. He was the descendant of another Becher, the second son of Ephraim ben Joseph. Somehow an ancestor of his had inherited the wealth of Ephraim's childless daughter Sheerah, the builder of cities who amassed a fortune. My broad estates were measured in terms of houses; his were cities.

Becher met us at his mansion just a mile south of Shechem. He stood by the gates of his manor, which was as large as many towns. Servants held pine torches for us.

"Greetings to my prospective son-in-law," he shouted heartily as we approached. "And to Heber the Kenite, who is welcome at my house."

In the flickering torchlight, I could see that Becher was dressed in a new white robe, trimmed in purple. I caught my breath. It looked exactly like mine, now lying folded in the donkey's pack.

I felt Heber's sly glance at me. He would be cynically amused. This could be awkward if I wore my white and purple robe tomorrow. I did not want to appear to be upstaging my father-in-law, as though I claimed to be as good as he. But I would have to wear it. Other than the travel-stained clothes I wore, I had no other garment.

Becher was a thoughtful and considerate host. In spite of the late hour of our arrival, he led us into his courtyard which was brightly lit by torches. Servants scurried everywhere making preparations for the wedding festivities tomorrow. Tables had been set up, ready to hold the large quantities of rich food and wine. Savory odors from the ovens pervaded the broad space.

It was too late for Becher to provide us with special entertainment, so he led us directly to our guest quarters. Heber and his men were given a large comfortable room on the second floor, and my men were established in a well-furnished suite on the east wing. Servants were assigned and baths prepared.

Then, having provided for the comfort of everyone else, he led me to the bridal chamber. There I would stay for the wedding week. The bridal chamber was actually a small house, built in the Canaanite style which our people had adopted since the conquest of our Promised Land.

We stepped through the gate into a small courtyard. A stairway led to the roof, with its sleeping quarters during this dry season. Just inside the house was a large commons room, whose outer wall marked the north end of Becher's estate. Everything was richly furnished — carpets on the floor, tapestries on the walls, soft couches, tables laden with bowls of fruit, and flowers everywhere. Lamps were lit, giving a homey glow to the house where I would bring my bride tomorrow night.

Becher bade me a warm welcome, then left me in the care of an aging servant couple, who were attentive and sensitive to my needs as I prepared for bed. I may have been abrupt with them as they meticulously washed my feet. I was tired and wanted only to sleep.

In the morning, I awakened at dawn as was my custom, although I had not been able to go to bed before midnight. Even here in the bridal chamber, so far from the main activities in the central courtyard, I could hear the bustle and clamor of the preparations for this festal day. I wondered how many people had been invited to the wedding. Since Becher was one of the most respected men in all the tribe of Ephraim, his guest list would be immense.

With some misgivings I put on my wedding garment, wondering if I should say anything to Becher about it. Would an apology be in order, or would it be more polite just to ignore the fact that my clothing would rival his in splendor? I decided my response would depend on Becher's reaction when I first confront him.

I strolled out of my house and walked toward the main courtyard. Last night I had not seen much, since it was so dark and we were exhausted. But now, even in the early light, I could see the vastness of the celebration.

The ovens in the southwestern corner still smoked, although their fires had been extinguished recently. Tables along the western edge were filled with food. They held several kinds of meat, fruits, nuts, puddings, vegetables, fresh bread, and cakes. One table contained nothing but wine, the containers reflecting brands from Egypt and Babylonia as well as the finest wine and beer from Becher's own vineyards and fields. Carpets had been spread on the bare courtyard. Incense burned in small vials, giving a faint sweet smell to the scene. Flowers in vases festooned the tables. Where did he find so many flowers in this dry season?

Servants bustled everywhere. They were all dressed alike — clean white robes, bound with a blue sash at the waist, and a white headpiece with a blue braided band to hold it in place.

At the table where the wine would be served, a young girl dressed in clean white supervised the servants. She was slim, her willowy body moving with quiet efficiency among the tables. No covering obscured her long dark hair. She looked up and saw me at about the same time I appeared among the tables. She hesitated a moment, smiled shyly, then turned and walked stiffly toward the large house where Becher lived.

I had just seen my bride. Deborah.

An ancient Israelite custom said that the groom should not see or speak to the bride on the wedding day. His first glimpse of her must be at the wedding ceremony, when he lifts the veil. Many Israelites pay little attention to this rather trivial custom, but I like to preserve all the traditions of Israel. Without firm traditions, our society would soon deteriorate.

Should I turn around and retreat to the bridal chamber, waiting until more people arrived? This would allow Deborah to come out and finish her work without embarrassment. I had no business being there so early.

None of the other guests were in sight. A few ladies of the household were there, supervising the servants. There were no men, other than several dark-skinned Nubians who did the heavy lifting. I should go back, and wait a while.

But I was hungry, and here was food. Before retreating, I would sample the cooking. Especially the meat, still juicy and warm from the ovens. And the bread, fresh-baked with an appetizing aroma. I approached the tables.

While I was enjoying my breakfast among the tables of food, I turned to see Becher coming out of his house. I was not surprised. Deborah would have told him I was here, and he would come out to speak to his most important guest.

And then I stared at him, my mouth open and a piece of bread halfway to my mouth. His clothing. His wedding garment. He was not wearing the white robe trimmed in purple which he wore last night. Instead, he wore a robe — equally white — but trimmed in gold!

Many of his guests today would be dressed in similar attire. Few would be able to afford purple. Why would he lay aside the rich robe he wore yesterday — and which I had assumed he would also wear for the main festivities — for this more common gold robe?

Only one reason suggested itself to me. He did not want to embarrass me. A thoughtful host, he would not try to place me in a position where I would be trying to imitate him. Therefore, since I would be the only person there wearing purple, I would be put at ease.

Someone must have told him I would be wearing purple. Who? Heber the Kenite? No, he had no chance, because he was shown directly to his quarters last night. My brother Rakem? He was here in the late afternoon yesterday — but Rakem paid no attention to these matters, and was most unlikely to even notice that we would both be wearing the same clothes. Who then?

As Becher approached me, I caught a glimpse behind him of Deborah, scurrying toward the women's quarters. She would be going there to put on her veil. Deborah? Could she have told her father that I was wearing purple?

No. She was only fourteen. Something like that would occur only to a mature, sensitive woman. A child would have no highly developed sense of thoughtful consideration and understanding of the feelings of others. It couldn't be.

2

"Yahweh bless you, Beriah ben Jonathan, my son."

"Yahweh bless you, Becher ben Ladan, my father."

When two traditional Israelite men greet each other, they always use the same formula. It shows good breeding and pride in the Israelite heritage.

"My house is yours." Becher continued his formal welcome with the ancient words of formal hospitality. "My servants are yours. My flocks and herds are yours. My food is yours. May you live long and prosper in the land Yahweh our God has given you."

"Thank you, my father. I am proud to be a part of your family."

Formalities now over, Becher led me to the wine table. Setting out two cups, he poured into them half water and half wine. That he would mix water and wine showed good sense; undiluted wine was consumed in the morning only by those who intended to get drunk before the day was over. That he would do the pouring himself, rather than ask a servant, honored me as his principal guest.

I sipped the wine. It was heavily spiced, delicious. My guess was it came from Damascus, world famous for fine beverages.

"Is there anything you need, my son?"

"You are thoughtful, father." I looked into his eyes, noting their youthful vigor. "I am sorry to bring you twenty-eight extra guests on such short notice."

Becher nodded, his brown beard thrust forward. "With Rakem's warning, we had no trouble preparing for them. He explained to us the, ah, circumstances."

I grinned. "And did Rakem tell you of his great love for the Kenite?"

Becher chuckled. "That he did, in great detail. Or rather, he did not tell me but Deborah."

"Oh?"

"Yes. It seems your brother and my daughter have become close friends in the few hours he was here last night before you arrived."

"Good." I took another sip of the spiced wine. "They will probably see a lot of each other in the future."

"Now, my son." Becher placed his wine cup on the table, untouched. I was glad to see my father-in-law was not much of a wine drinker. "What are your needs today? How may I serve you?"

I too placed my cup on the table. I had promised myself to drink sparingly on my wedding day. "I have a request, father, but not for myself. For Heber, and his Kenite men. They have come to this feast without wedding garments. Do you have some proper clothes you could lend them for this day? I would not have them embarrass you."

"You are thoughtful, my son." Becher smiled. "That was taken care of last night. Early this morning, twenty-eight robes were delivered to the guest room upstairs where the Kenites are quartered."

"Really?" I looked at my father-in-law with new respect. "You are shrewd to anticipate their needs."

He laughed. "In all honesty, Beriah, it was not I who thought of that. It was your betrothed."

"Deborah?" I stared at him.

"Deborah." He nodded. "I shall miss her. Since her mother died two years ago, Deborah has managed this household. You will find she'll make a perfect wife."

"Deborah." I looked in the direction of the house into which my bride had gone to find a veil. I felt a wave of emotion flooding my body. My eyes filled. I recalled the ancient proverb which I heard from my father Jonathan: "A virtuous wife, who can find? Her price is beyond gold and silver."

I took a deep breath, controlling my emotions. "My father, I have a gift for you."

"A gift? That's not necessary, Beriah. Your father paid the bride-price long ago."

"I know." I always wondered what the bride-price was, whether large or small. My father never told me. I continued, "Nevertheless I have a gift for you not measured in material terms. I wrote a poem in your honor."

"Ah!" He smiled broadly and seemed genuinely pleased.

I had not been sure of his reaction. Many men — like Heber the Kenite — regarded poetry as something done by weak men with nothing better to do in their spare time. Especially empty poetry. An inspiring singer who composed both music and lyrics was virile and respected, but an empty poet was considered effeminate. I pulled the scroll from the folds of my garment and handed it to him.

He unrolled it eagerly. "This needs to be sung."

I bit my lip. An insult? No, Becher would never do that. Then what did he mean?

He looked at me, smiling. "I shall have

this sung today by the sweetest singer in all Israel. I am most grateful."

His words reassured me. Far from insulting me, he was offering to have my poem enhanced by a competent singer and composer. He seemed to be saying that the poetry was well worth setting to music.

He excused himself and went to one of his servant girls, and spoke to her briefly. I saw him hand my scroll to her, and she left.

Then he returned. "This afternoon," he said. "At the feast. Your poem shall be given a place of honor."

"Thank you."

Now guests began to arrive at Becher's gate. He went to greet them, and I was left alone to watch the proceedings. There was little for me to do, since I was a guest.

Becher's house reflected the ways and customs of a traditional Israelite. For the wedding festivities, all the animals inside the walls of his large manor had been driven out into the field. Every inch was scrubbed and swept and polished. Flowers were everywhere, and well-dressed, well-trained servants were eager to make the visitors comfortable in all ways.

The guests as they arrived were introduced to me. I knew most of them by reputation. All the Ephraimites I knew personally, and some of the men of Manassah. Several other tribes were represented also.

A small orchestra played traditional Israelite music, moving from one part of the large courtyard to another. I was pleased to see a group of Levite singers. This ceremony would be properly honored by a psalm or two.

Before long the large courtyard was crowded and noisy. Old friends shouted greetings to each other. As the wine was consumed, the talk became boisterous, even raucous. Many of the men drank too much, but that also seemed to be one of the traditions of Israel, although I would have preferred my wedding day to be more sedate.

Heber and his Kenites appeared before long, dressed in their borrowed wedding garments. They wore a variety of colors — gold, blue, orange, yellow, brown. On such short notice Becher would not be able to round up twenty-eight robes of the same color. It was a minor miracle that he had found twenty-eight robes.

Rakem appeared, looking uncomfortable in his white robe trimmed in brown. He made a conscious effort to avoid Heber, for which I was grateful. Maybe Becher had cautioned him last night to act as a guest should in his house.

Deborah herself mingled with the guests, although her head was covered in a thick white veil. Some brides of Israel would have stayed inside through the whole day, soaking their bodies in perfumed bath water; washing, oiling, and brushing their hair; selecting baubles and necklaces to wear. My bride had obviously dressed for the day early and spent the entire morning greeting the guests, supervising the servants, making sure the wine jars were filled. I saw her talking with Heber, and later with Rakem. They seemed to be attracted to her. They laughed often, or listened respectfully when she spoke to them.

Through the long day she avoided me. This was proper. No Israelite bride should speak to the groom on her wedding day.

In the afternoon, Becher led the male guests out through the gates of his house to a hilltop where he had set up an altar. There he offered a prime bullock and seven sheep, following the tradition of sacrificial worship established in the time of Abraham. One of the Levites cut the throats of the beasts. This too was proper in Israelite tradition; that was why the Levites were scattered among the tribes and accepted as permanent guests in houses such as Becher's.

Although Heber and Rakem glared at

each other, they made no attempt to renew their argument. I stood with Rakem during the sacrifice and returned to the house with him. Heber preferred the company of his Kenites.

When we returned, the tables had been replenished with freshly cooked meat, hot bread, new puddings, and much wine. We sat down to the traditional "marriage feast," one of the highlights of the wedding festivities.

As the level of the wine jars went down, the noise level went up. The guests shouted to one another, sang ribald songs, told long rambling stories, boasted of great deeds, and generally became obnoxious. I suppose I would not have been aware of this had I been drinking heavily myself. But since I was not, all the celebration seemed to me excessive debauchery.

Throughout the feast, the orchestra played. The lyres, flutes, timbrel, and horns were drowned out by the raucous festivity. I hoped Becher would forget about having his special singer perform my poem. A serious composition, it would be profaned by this drunken crowd.

Becher had obviously drunk very little and seemed less inebriated than most of his guests. Rising, he called for silence. It took several minutes for the guests to quiet enough for him to be heard.

"My friends," he shouted. "We have a special treat in store. Our honored guest," and here he indicated me with a wave of his hand, "has written a poem for this occasion."

His announcement was greeted with cheers and shouts of laughter. I frowned. This was not a good audience for my solemn poem.

And then I saw her. Deborah. My bride. She came from one of the houses, walking slowly toward the center of the tables. Her wedding dress and heavy veil gleamed like the snow on Mount Hermon on a sunny day.

She carried a lyre.

No! Not her! Not here, not now, not in this crowd! Not with my poem!

She stopped in front of the orchestra, the only woman in sight. She stood there, tall and quiet, waiting for the right moment.

To my amazement, the guests began to get quiet. They sat on their benches, gazing at her, waiting. The momentum of silence swept the courtyard.

She strummed the lyre, and the dulcet tones contrasted sharply with the clamor of a moment ago. She sang,

Blessing in the city,
Blessing in the field,
Blessing on the battle ground,
Blessing in the home;
    These belong to the man
    Whose mind is set on Yahweh.

Such a man is Becher,
Son of Ladan, of Ephraim.
Fairest of ten thousand,
Who shines among the stars.
    He is the strength of Israel,
    He is a man of God.

May all the sons of Israel
Stand with this man of might.
May all the sons of Abraham
Walk tall and pure and free.
    Thus will the Land of Promise
    Be ours through all the years.

There was more, of course. She sang with a clear sweet voice. The song was melodious, wistful, yet filled with energy. And she sang to a silent, rapt audience. With a final chord, she finished. She bowed her head to indicate the song was over. Still a hush pervaded the courtyard.

Then suddenly the spell was broken, and the cheers broke out. They yelled, they shouted, they roared. Some waved their arms; several stood and banged their fists on the table.

The figure in white turned and pointed to me. Instantly the attention of the guests turned in my direction, and they whooped and cheered, lifting their wine glasses. I think I was the only one who saw my bride quietly slip out of the crowd and disappear into one of the houses.

I sat there, stunned. I must have had a stupid expression on my face, because many of the men were laughing at me. But it was good-natured laughter; I knew they appreciated my poem.

I had thought it was quite ordinary . . . until this moment. The music had enriched it beyond anything I could have imagined. Suddenly a mediocre poem had become a beautiful and resplendent song.

Sung by my bride. My Deborah. My wife and future companion. The first of my poems ever put to music.

The first. But surely not the last.

3

The wedding procession, intended as a happy occasion for the groom, almost turned into a disaster.

We gathered at the bridal chamber, where Deborah and I would spend our first night. The courtyard was crowded. There were Rakem, my brother, and the men I had brought from Bethel; Heber and his Kenites; and a few other men of the tribe of Ephraim who considered themselves friends of my family. The courtyard was small, the groom's party large.

I was still inside, oiling my hair and beard while the two elderly servants arranged my wedding garments so the folds draped in the right place and the hem came to just above the ankles. The woman servant tied the sash around my waist while the man fastened the straps of my sandals. I ran the comb through my hair and beard. I was eager to make a good impression on my bride.

That was when it happened. Angry voices in the courtyard just outside the door caused me to drop my comb and run outside, one leather string of my sandal still untied.

Rakem and Heber stood there, glaring at each other, while around them the large crowd of men shouted and took sides.

I pushed through the crowd and stood between them. "Stop it!" I barked. "This is my wedding night!"

Heber nodded and spoke through clenched teeth. "That's why this pig brother of yours is still alive, Beriah. Only because I respect the peace of this house."

"Some day," said Rakem softly, "when my brother is not getting married, you and I will settle this."

"Yes." Heber turned his eyes from my brother and looked at me. "Some day, Beriah, I will cut the tail off this stupid pig."

"But not my wedding night." My voice was as firm as possible, trying to include both Heber and Rakem in my reprimand. "At least respect the house of Becher, where we are guests. This is a wedding feast, not a brawl."

The men in the courtyard had grown silent. For a tense moment, nothing was said. Then Heber sighed. "All right. No fighting. For your sake. And for the sake of your lovely bride."

Rakem took a deep breath. "Yes. For

Deborah and Beriah. Let there be peace."

I looked from one to the other. A fragile truce held them apart. Both were drunk. How much longer could this go on?

"Let's go," I said.

I led the wedding procession, with Rakem on my right and Heber on my left. We went out the gate from the small courtyard of the bridal chamber and into the broad open yard of Becher's manor.

The tables had been taken down, except for a few wine tables in a corner. Oil lamps and torches cast an eerie flickering light across the courtyard. People were everywhere; men from all the tribes had gathered for the wedding procession. Along the west wall, the Levite singers began a wedding chant, which sounded like a cross between a psalm of praise to Yahweh and a love song appropriate to the marriage bed. That these two themes could be combined so cleverly was a tribute to some creative musician in Becher's household.

The wine consumed during the long day of feasting had taken its toll. The revelers were not interested in the quarrel between Rakem and Heber. Their shouts and ribald jibes almost drowned out the Levite's chant. I think I was the only sober man in the courtyard that night.

The procession from my house, as symbolized by the bridal chamber where I stayed, to the bride's house — Becher's quarters where Deborah waited — seemed long. Actually it was only a few hundred paces. I was supposed to walk slowly, so the revelers could make their bawdy shouts. Instead I walked faster. I wanted to get this part over with, and send these drunken fools to their beds. And of course bring Deborah to my bed.

Becher stood at the entrance to his living quarters. Just inside the gate, in the inner courtyard about the size of the one where I was staying, his relatives and close friends had gathered. I saw beside him his son-in-law, Ezer, who had married Deborah's older sister. Becher had no sons; Ezer would probably inherit his wealth, although part of it might come to me. I was pleased to see that Becher was sober. At least this part of the ceremony would be dignified, following the ancient customs of Israel.

The crowd grew silent in preparation for Becher's speech. Sometimes the father of the bride would take this occasion to make a long oration, or play on the crowd with vulgar humor. But I did not expect Becher to act like that. Especially since he was sober. I was not disappointed.

"Beriah ben Jonathan, my son." His voice

boomed out across the crowd. Nobody would fail to hear him tonight.

"I give you my daughter, Deborah. She is my second child, the offspring of the union between myself and my beloved wife, Milcah. The betrothal contract was made by myself and your father Jonathan many years ago. A satisfactory bride-price was paid. I certify that she is a virgin."

These last words, required in the traditional marriage ceremony, brought whoops and laughter from the assembled men. Someone behind me shouted, "Prove it!" This was a standard wedding joke among drunken guests. Sometimes they made the absurd demand to examine the bed sheets in the morning. I have never quite approved of this uncouth reaction in a drunken crowd, but it was a part of the marriage tradition. And who am I to deny tradition?

When the crowd quieted enough for Becher to continue, he spoke solemnly. "May Yahweh give you many sons, Beriah. Strong, healthy boys who will grow into men, who will keep you in safety through all your long and prosperous years."

I detected a wistfulness in this last statement, as though Becher were covering his own regret that he himself had no sons. He would want many grandsons, of course;

they would "keep him in safety" throughout his old age. I resolved that I would respect his unspoken plea. My father-in-law would always have my support and protection as he grew older.

"And now, my son," Becher concluded. "You may take your bride to your bed."

It was over; a relatively short speech. The guests again broke out in loud shouts and laughter, bawling their crude jokes at the top of their voices.

"Take her, Beriah!"

"Make your marriage bed in the court-yard, man!"

"Be sure you peek under her veil!"

The last was a reference to an old joke in Israel, referring to our ancestor Jacob, who was given the wrong bride by concealing her under a heavy veil. It had given rise to the wedding custom which was now my next task.

I strode into the inner courtyard of Becher's living quarters. A path opened among the family gathered there so that I could enter the house. Inside, in the flickering lamplight, I saw Deborah standing alone against the far wall. She was gleaming in white.

Ignoring the racy shouts of the drunken crowd outside, I walked slowly toward my bride. Gently I lifted the long veil. She looked at me meekly, her thin lips quivering in a shy smile.

Tenderly I kissed her cheek and whispered in her ear, "Yahweh bless you, wife."

Traditional words. They required no answer, or at the very least an equally traditional response such as, "And you too, husband."

But Deborah's reply was different. "My husband. May you be as the man in your poem."

I looked into her eyes, and she gazed back steadily. Somehow a spark of understanding flashed between us. I smiled. This would be an idyllic union.

I carefully replaced the veil and took her hand, leading her out of the house and into the crowd. The procession to our bridal chambers would be a long one.

I felt the pressure of her hand in mine as we made our way slowly along the small aisle they had cleared for us. Around us arose a chorus of crude suggestions about what we should do in the bridal chambers. We could not hear the Levite singers. We could hear nothing, in fact, but the drunken din. Forgetting the tradition that the marriage procession should be slow, we began to hurry.

At the gates of our chambers, I turned to the crowd. "This is where I say good night to you, my friends," I shouted. Then I shut the gates in their faces.

"No! Not now, Beriah!"

"Let us in!"

"Do you need any help?"

The gates were sturdy. I took my bride's hand and led her into the house.

4

I led Deborah into the commons of the small house which was our bridal chamber. The elderly slave couple had actually prepared two places for us to spend the night — here, and upstairs on the roof. It might be somewhat cooler upstairs, but I knew that before the night was over the dampness and chill would make us wish we had stayed down here.

"Would you like something to drink?" I asked, indicating the table of drinks and food prepared for us.

"Yes, I would."

Deborah began to lift the heavy veil from her head. I went to her and helped her take it off. She folded it carefully and laid it on a table.

The lamplight flickered on her face. She ran her hand over her straight hair. The black strands were freshly oiled and combed, although removing the veil had tousled it a little. She had a thin face, high cheekbones, and a small mouth which now smiled self-consciously at me. Before she lowered her eyes, I noticed they were very dark, although I couldn't be sure of the color in the dim light.

I went to the table and reached for the small pitcher of water. We seated ourselves on the bench at a table. I felt as awkward as she probably did. Neither of us was experienced in the activity which lay ahead of us. While I looked forward to it in a vague, pleasurable way, I felt clumsy and stupid about how to initiate it. So we just sat there, sipping our drinks, our embarrassment deepening.

Deborah was the one who spoke first. "Thank you for staying sober today. It was thoughtful of you."

I wondered how to respond to her. I had to say something. So I blundered on with the first thought that came to my mind. "And thank you for telling your father that I was wearing purple."

She smiled, staring at her cup. "I . . . I didn't want you to be embarrassed."

So it *was* her! But . . . she looked so much like a little girl. How could she possibly be that mature and sensitive? The silence between us was heavy and seemed to be pushing us apart. We needed to find a topic of conversation which would bring us together.

"Tell me," I said, groping for a subject, "were there many Becherites at the wedding today?"

"Oh yes." She seemed eager to find a topic which would relieve the awkwardness between us. "There were about twenty of father's relatives."

"Becherites" was what everyone called the descendants of the first Becher, son of Ephraim. I was familiar with their history, but if I pretended ignorance, perhaps she would talk freely and relax a little.

"Your father," I said slowly, "is the most prominent among them. I have heard of your ancestor Sheerah. Didn't she build a city?"

"She built three cities. Lower and Upper Beth-horon and Uzzen-Sheerah. She had no descendants, and my ancestor Becher inherited her wealth."

I knew all that, and I suspect she knew I knew. She gave me a brief smile, as though she understood that I was merely trying to put her at ease.

"Now tell me something about yourself," she said. "And why are you named as you are?" (My name in our language means "misery.")

"I was named for the youngest son of Ephraim," I replied. "Are you familiar with his story?"

"Only vaguely. Tell me." I suspected she knew more than she let on, but, like me, she was encouraging me to talk.

"Our ancestor, Ephraim ben Joseph, had many sons. Two of them, Elead and Ezer, stole some cattle from the Canaanites. But later in another raid both were killed. Ephraim took it very hard, mourning them for many days. When finally his wife conceived and bore him his last son, Ephraim named him Beriah."

Deborah looked at me, her eyes wide. "But why did your father name you that? Why would he want to give his only legitimate son and heir a name which means 'misery?' "

"It wasn't my father who named me. It was my mother. Zebiah. My birth was difficult for her." I shrugged. "You'll meet her in a few days."

"Good. I'm looking forward to it."

"I have arranged for you to live in my house at Ramah. My mother Zebiah lives in Bethel."

"But Beriah, I would love to share your mother's home in Bethel. Why can't I?"

"She's . . . well, she's hard to get along with."

"Why?"

I shrugged. "She has a . . . well, let's say

she's not well. I don't know how to explain it. Not many people get along with her. Father couldn't. That's why he built the house in Bethel for her. So he could live at Ramah in peace."

"Oh. I see." She frowned. I noticed the sharp creases on her forehead between her eyes. This was the first time I had ever seen her frown.

"Beriah, I still want to live with her. At least in the beginning. Let me try, will you?"

"Why?"

She shrugged. "I don't know. She's your mother. And my mother now. My real mother died two years ago. I miss her."

Her voice was soft and pleading. A child's voice. How could I refuse her?

"All right. We'll go there first. For a few days. Then you can decide whether you want to live with Zebiah in Bethel or move to the house at Ramah. I think I know what your decision will be."

"I don't understand." Again the little pout in her frown appeared between her eyes. "Zebiah. How can someone whose name means 'gazelle' be so . . . so . . . sad?"

"She looks like a gazelle. Pretty. Graceful. But what a person looks like on the outside isn't always what she looks like inside."

Deborah smiled; her eyes lit up. "I know.

You, for example. You don't look like a person whose name means 'misery.' "

I laughed. "Maybe that's because I have been trying too hard all my life *not* to live up to my name."

She joined in my laughter. But as our laughter died away, the awkward silence once again hung between us.

"You are a very thoughtful husband," she murmured. "Not only did you stay sober on our wedding day, but you have tried to put me at ease tonight. Thank you."

She reached over and placed her hand on mine, a small gesture of affection. I grasped her hand and pulled her closer to me. She came willingly. With my other hand, I lifted her chin and placed a tender kiss on her lips.

"Deborah," I whispered. "I shall be as gentle as I can."

She smiled. "I know, my husband. You are that kind of a person."

The lovemaking which followed was awkward, but I did try to be as gentle as possible. I could tell that it was painful for her, although she tried her best not to show it. I had heard — and surely she knew this too — that it was painful for a virgin only on the first night. I would not have put her through this, but I knew it was necessary. Her main task in life was to give me sons, and there was no other way to do it.

My own enjoyment of the conjugal act was muted because I knew the agony I caused my bride. She was so frail, so helpless, and so innocent. I was in no small anguish myself because of what I was doing to her.

Perhaps it would be better tomorrow night. For both of us.

5

The old slave couple came to the bridal chambers at dawn. I had just awakened, and I let them in the gate. Deborah was still asleep.

They had brought with them fresh fruit and bread for our breakfast, as well as clean clothing. I sent the woman into the house to help Deborah bathe and dress, while I put on the linen tunic I had worn when I traveled here. The servant had cleaned and brushed it.

When Deborah was dressed, I sent the old couple away and barred the gates. The manor was quiet in the early morning, but soon it would be bustling again with more of the mindless drinking and celebration which is a part of a wedding feast. Deborah and I were entitled to a week of peace. I intended to keep the doors barred for the entire week, letting in only the servants who had promised to come each morning at dawn.

The bread was freshly baked and still warm. Of the fruit they had brought, I preferred the dried figs and dates, while Deborah's taste ran toward juicy fruits. She handled a knife skillfully as she chopped up a pomegranate and sucked its juicy flesh.

"Now, Deborah," I said as I laid aside the bowl of dried figs. "We should talk."

She smiled, charmingly. I noticed a smudge of pomegranate on her face.

I continued. "About marriage. About the duties of a wife to her husband."

She nodded. "I will try to be a good wife to you. Always."

"Good. I want the house kept spotlessly clean. There will be many servants, which you will supervise in their daily tasks. And the gardening. And marketing. I like fresh vegetables. I will not always be home, but —" I paused, frowning. A grin had spread over her face.

"What is it?" I asked. "Is something funny?"

She laughed. "No. I don't think so. But. . . ." She wiped the smudge of pomegranate from her face. "I just had an image in my mind of you beating me because I served you yesterday's bread for breakfast. You wouldn't do that, would you?" And again she laughed.

At first I wondered if she were mocking me. But I rejected that. She would not do that. She was merely a child, full of good humor and elfish enthusiasm. Besides, her laughter was infectious.

I too laughed. "Every day," I said. "With a stout oak staff."

That was the way our conversation went throughout the entire day. We talked long and often about our relationship, our home, our family. Every once in a while she would break into the seriousness of our discussion with laughter and humor. I think those times occurred only when I began to get too pompous and overbearing, or — because of my age, wisdom, and vast experience — too patronizing. Yet never did she make me feel inferior. Always, without exception, I was the ruler of our house, and she was the wife.

But I couldn't escape the thought that, in her own subtle way, she could lead me through decisions and difficulties and problems. Not by orders and demands as I would. But with delicately deceptive ruses, made acceptable to me by humor and laughter. As for example when we talked about having children.

"I want lots of sons, Deborah. Good, strong, healthy sons. I want you to be for me what Leah was to Jacob."

"Do you want twelve?" she asked, her mouth twitching.

"It doesn't have to be exactly twelve," I said. "But a goodly number."

"And how many daughters do you want, if any?"

"It doesn't matter. As long as there are sons."

"And if I give you more daughters than sons, will you beat me?"

It was then I realized she was using her subtle wiles on me. I wondered why I didn't resent it. Instead, I laughed. "For every daughter," I said, "I will beat you only with a hickory switch. Until the number of daughters exceeds the number of sons. Then I will beat you with an oak staff."

In later years I would look back on this conversation and marvel at her subtlety. Somehow she had just told me that God determines the number and sex of children, not the wife, no matter how much she wants to please her husband.

And she had also somehow established that I would not beat her. Wife-beating was a common practice among the Canaanites and evidently the Kenites. Although it was permitted in the law of Moses, it was seldom practiced. I had never seen my father beat anyone. I knew I would not be capable of beating a wife — especially this charming child whose face radiated serenity and trust in my presence. She had the uncanny ability to make me feel at ease with her, while at the same time not allowing me to be egotistical and condescending.

Several times during the day and evening we were interrupted by shouts and pounding on the gates by drunken revelers. We ignored them.

Once I distinguished the harsh voice of Heber the Kenite. "Let me in, Beriah. I want to make sure she's not a virgin any more!" Our silence from inside soon discouraged him, and he went away.

The second night was indeed better than the first. This time there was no pain, and she seemed not only willing but eager. Our lovemaking was tender as well as ardent, solicitous of each other's feelings and enjoyment. We seemed to blend our souls as well as our bodies.

The next morning we left our bed only long enough to receive our servants at dawn, who helped us bathe and then cleaned the house. After they left we returned to our blissful pursuits.

About midmorning we were startled by a loud knocking at the gates. I thought at first it was the drunken revelers, even at that hour. But then I heard Becher's voice. I knew something was wrong.

I hastily put on my tunic and ran through the courtyard to unbar the gate. Becher stood there, his hair and beard unoiled and uncombed.

"Beriah, there's been some trouble!"

I felt my stomach turn. "Rakem and Heber?"

"Yes. I kept them apart yesterday. But. . . ."

"What is it, Becher? Where are they now?"

"I don't know. They're gone. So are all the Kenites." He took a deep breath. "So are all your men."

I knew immediately what had happened. Their quarrel had come into focus. Now they were settling it in deadly combat, somewhere outside the bounds of Becher's house. Neither of them would insult their host by fighting here, but neither of them had thought through the consequences of their rashness. They were blinded by their rage. And no doubt by too much wine.

"Do you know where they went?" I asked.

"No. I posted men on all the high places of my house to look for them."

"Good. If they are near by, they'll see them."

As fast as I could, I fastened my sandals and threw on my outer cloak, tightening the leather belt. Then I went with Becher to the main courtyard just outside his quarters.

"Any sign of them?" Becher shouted to the men whom I could see standing on the tops of houses and along the outer wall, shading their eyes as they gazed off into the distance.

No one answered. That meant they were not in sight. I could feel the muscles in my neck and shoulders tightening. I started to pace but stopped because it would mean turning my back on Becher.

If only I had gone out yesterday and talked to Rakem. And Heber. He seemed to respect me, even when he was drunk. Perhaps he would have listened. I should have anticipated that this would happen. But it did no good to blame myself. I must think about what to do now.

Immediately I rejected the idea of rushing out to search for them. I had no idea which direction they went. If I went north and they went south, nothing would be accomplished. No, better to wait until someone on the walls and rooftops sighted something.

Waiting was the hardest thing in the world to do. Couldn't I do something? Perhaps send out some men to look for them, sending them in all directions, fast runners, to report back to me as soon as they found them.

I turned to Becher to present my plan, but

before I could say anything, someone on the north wall shouted, "Someone's coming!"

"Where?" I demanded.

The man on the wall pointed. "From the north. There are several men. I think . . . ten. No, eleven. One seems to be carrying something."

My stomach churned. "No, Yahweh, no!" I muttered, running toward the small door on the north wall of the estate.

They were still several hundred paces away from Becher's house, but I continued running toward them. Even before I was close enough to see clearly, I heard them.

They were wailing.

Modan, Rakem's son, was carrying a body. And I knew whose body it was, even before I drew close enough to see.

I stopped, fifty paces from them. I grasped the top of my linen tunic and ripped it. I stooped and caught up a handful of dirt and threw it on my head. As I did so, I became aware of my own voice. And my tears.

Modan was struggling under the heavy burden, but he would not allow his men to help him. I understood why. His father. But he did allow me, the brother of the dead man, to take the body and carry it the rest of the way to Becher's house.

Becher had torn the beautiful gold and

white wedding garment which he wore. Dust covered his hair and beard. He wailed and beat his breast, as did everyone else in the courtyard as I entered.

Gently I laid the body of my brother at his feet. Then I stood, my feet straddling the body, and raised my hands for silence. They respected my wish, knowing what was to come.

I filled my lungs and shouted. "I claim the right of the avenger! According to the law of Moses, Rakem's blood is now on my hands. I swear before Yahweh and all these witnesses that before I die I shall see the blood of Heber the Kenite spill on the ground!"

Shouts of approval and anger arose from the crowd gathered around me. Everybody was there now — all of Becher's household, and all the wedding guests who remained. They knew as well as I the law of Moses: *If a man is struck down and killed by a metal weapon, his killer is a murderer and shall be put to death. The avenger of blood shall personally put the murderer to death when he meets him.*

It was the law. It was my obligation to my family. I knew it, and everyone there knew it. And now I had sworn my solemn oath before Yahweh.

Even in my grief and anger, a part of my mind was functioning smoothly. I thought of Modan, young and inexperienced, burning with desire for revenge. By speaking the oath of the avenger first, I had probably saved him from dashing off impulsively to do battle with the more experienced Heber.

And that thought caused little tingles of fear to creep up and down my spine. The more experienced Heber. I was no match for him myself. I was not a fighter. Rakem was a far better warrior than I, and Heber had struck him down. What could I do?

But I knew there was a way. There had to be. A way that did not call for face-to-face, man-to-man combat. A way to match my intelligence and cunning against his strength and martial skills. There was a way. I would find it.

I had sworn an oath to Yahweh in the presence of witnesses to be my brother's blood avenger. And I meant to fulfill that oath.

6

I told Becher, as politely as I could, that we would start for home immediately. He agreed. The wedding was over. There was nothing more to celebrate.

There was little to do in preparation for our journey. I sent a runner ahead to tell my household to prepare for the funeral. Becher loaned us a span of oxen and a cart on which we laid the body. Then he embraced his daughter, spoke brief words of farewell to me, and waved good-bye from the gates of his manor.

Because we started so late in the day, and also because our pace was set by the lumbering oxen, we arrived at the estate just outside Bethel in the middle of the second night. The house was dark. They did not expect us to come after dark.

Our shouts aroused the servants, who lit torches, then went to awaken my mother Zebiah. She dressed hastily and met us in the courtyard. She wore a clean dress. Even in the flickering torchlight I could see it was not torn. She had not been mourning.

Mother approached us, frowning. Her pretty, youthful face seemed to reflect her disposition. Very seldom have I seen her smiling.

She gave me a perfunctory kiss, and without even a word of greeting, began her scolding. "Why didn't you tell us you were coming in the middle of the night? We weren't expecting you so soon. You could at least have told that boy who brought news of your brother's death when you would come. We're not ready for you. There's a lot to do before the funeral. When is it going to be? Today, I hope. You know how bodies stink when they aren't buried immediately. But if it's to be today, we'll have to get word out to all the families —"

"Mother," I said sharply, cutting into her diatribe. "This is my bride, Deborah. She's very tired. We all are. Please see that she gets to bed for a few hours sleep. I'll handle all the funeral arrangements."

Zebiah glanced at Deborah, who came forward hesitantly. Mother looked into her face. "She's very young, Beriah. Is she ready to give you children?"

Deborah's drawn face lit up with a smile. "Mother Zebiah, how good to meet you." She reached out with both hands and grasped Mother's. "We have lots to talk about. But I'm so tired. Please show me where I can sleep."

"Well . . . I suppose you can sleep in the north guest room. Will Beriah be with you, or will you be alone?"

I spoke up then. "She'll be alone. For tonight. I'll be busy making funeral arrangements."

"Well, come along, child. But you won't get much sleep tonight, I'm afraid, since you arrived so unexpectedly in the middle of the night. But we'll see what we can do. . . ."

Together they went across the courtyard toward the north end of the house. The bedroom she designated for Deborah was a guest room. I wondered what Mother would say when she learned that her new daughter-in-law planned to make her permanent residence here.

There was much to do in preparation for the funeral. I selected several young men from the households at Bethel to deliver messages to all the near relatives throughout Ephraim. We would meet here today at noon, and the funeral procession would proceed through the city of Bethel to our family burial grounds on the ridge east of that city.

Modan and I bathed and dressed Rakem's

body and placed it on the bier which we would carry in the funeral procession. In the early dawn, people began to arrive at our house. The wailing began.

A family in mourning follows certain customs which originated in years past, beyond the memory of anyone. The wailing must be continuous. As a boy, I found some fascination in trying to distinguish between the high-pitched keening of women and the bass or tenor moaning of men. Everyone developed sore throats and afterward spoke in whispers or croaks.

The people who arrived at the Bethel house, all well-known to me, wore their clothing in rags. They were appropriately dirty, having strewn dust on their heads and faces. Very few words were spoken; instead everyone tried to keep up the continuous wailing. We could eat or drink nothing, which only added to the misery of our sore throats. In the heat of the day, people occasionally fainted as they stood for hours under the bright sun. Tradition. A few minor inconveniences were unimportant, as long as the strong ties of tradition bound us together.

Reverently we placed Rakem's body in a tomb on the ridge east of Bethel, where he would lie with our father Jonathan forever.

His mothers were buried there also — both his legal mother and his natural mother. His wife Tamar would be buried there too, and probably fairly soon, since she was in poor health.

When we came out of the tomb on the ridge, the large throng of mourners was quiet. Not a word was spoken as we made our way down the hillside and separated at Bethel to go to our individual homes. Deborah joined me, but we could not speak until sundown. Tradition forbade it.

The hours seemed long until sunset. We were thirsty. And hungry. I had eaten nothing since breakfast the previous morning. We sat on the rooftop watching the sun make its sluggish journey toward the western hills. Not until it had disappeared and the shofar sounded did I permit wine to be poured. Nothing ever tasted so good.

Deborah slept that night in the north guest room, while I slept on the roof. Again, tradition. We could not have sexual relations for three days after the burial. This was proper, out of respect for the deceased.

In spite of my exhaustion, I awoke at dawn. No one else was up, so I slipped out the gate and walked to my favorite spot, where I had spent many boyhood hours. About half a mile to the south, on the much-traveled road to Ramah, I came to a hollow in the hills out of which ran a small stream across the road. Following the path along the stream about twenty paces, I came to the spring, where it bubbled up from the hillside. Pine trees surrounded the glen, spreading their soft green arms like a benediction. Their needles on the ground made a rich carpet, and their fragrance was like the finest incense.

In the center of the glen grew a palm tree. No one had ever explained how a palm tree could grow in this terrain, but there it was. An act of God, some said. Its tall slender stem reached toward the sky and the fronds pointed like graceful arms in all directions.

I had come here often in the past. When my family wanted to look for me, this is where they started. Sometimes they referred to this place as "Beriah's Palm Tree."

Underneath this tree some thoughtful person long years ago had built a stone bench. There I sat, as I had so often in the past, enjoying the morning. Sunlight filtered through the pine trees in the east, bathing the glen in a soft green glow. The only noise was the quiet bubbling of the spring as it burst from its rocky hillside about ten paces away.

How often in years gone by I had sat here

and dreamed. Composed poetry. Laid grandiose plans. Found peace. Here I would bring Deborah. I was sure she would love this place.

I knew I must be about the business of planning my brother's revenge. Somehow, I must organize an expedition to seek out Heber and fulfill my vow. But I couldn't plan it this morning. Not with that lark singing so proudly in the pine tree. Not with the gentle morning air caressing my face. Not with the brook whispering to me of peace.

Peace. I closed my eyes and breathed deeply.

As so often happened, my mind drifted into a composition of a poem.

> Praise Yahweh, O my soul.
> Praise him on the mountain.
> Praise him in the deepest valleys.
> Praise him beside the still waters.
> Praise him. . . .

Suddenly I sat upright, my eyes wide open. I had just remembered something. No longer did I need to compose empty poetry. Now . . . now . . . there was a voice who could sing it.

This called for a slight change in wording.

71

Sing praises to Yahweh, O my soul.
Sing praises to him on the mountain.
Sing praises to him in the deepest valleys.
Sing praises to him beside the still waters.
O my soul, sing praises to Yahweh,
   for he is good,
   his love endures forever.

The words took shape in my mind and I could almost hear the silver voice of my wife challenging the sweet song of the lark in the pine tree. The tiredness left my body, and I rose from the bench. With a spring in my step I walked toward my house.

When Deborah awoke for the day, I would bring her here. I would share with her the beauty and serenity of this place. And together we would make music to rival that bird's.

7

As I walked through the gates of my manor into the courtyard, I was surprised to see Deborah in serious conversation with Rakem's son Modan. They looked like a pair of children talking somberly about something in their play. Perhaps I should have felt a twinge of jealousy, since Modan was closer to her age than I was, but curiously I did not. What I felt was a fatherly concern for both of them.

They turned to me eagerly as soon as they saw me.

"Beriah," said Modan, his voice barely concealing his anxiety. "Mother's very sick. I think she's dying."

Rakem's frail wife had not attended the burial yesterday. Their home was my other manor at Ramah.

I said, "Losing her husband would be a shock to her. And perhaps a little fear, also. Please assure her that as long as she lives, she will be well cared for in my house."

Modan nodded. "We know that, Beriah. It's not just that. It's the fever. . . ."

"Fever? Perhaps I should send Jehoaddah to heal her."

Jehoaddah was our family's *rophe,* whose outdated methods of healing were more superstition than medical arts. He was old, and as soon as he died, I planned to replace him with an Egyptian trained in the House of Life at Thebes.

"Thank you." Modan glanced quickly at my wife. "But . . . can Deborah come too? A woman's touch. . . ."

"Please, Beriah." Deborah stepped to my side, placing her hand into mine. "I think I can help her. I have nursed women before."

I frowned. I didn't want to be separated from my wife so early in our marriage. I wanted to show her my palm tree and teach her the words of my new poem so she could compose a tune for it. But that would have to wait. I could not decently refuse this request. Modan's mother needed a woman's gentle hand to help with her healing.

Two more nights of celibacy lay ahead of me anyway, because of the funeral traditions. It might be easier if I knew Deborah were not in the same house with me.

"All right," I said. "Modan, take twenty-seven household guards. I don't want Deborah on the road to Ramah without a strong escort."

He nodded, as much aware as I of the danger of roaming Canaanite bands. "Thank you, Beriah," he murmured, then turned and ran toward the barracks where the guards were quartered.

Deborah tightened her hand in mine and looked into my eyes. "You are thoughtful and kind," she said softly. "I will miss you."

I squeezed her hand. "And I will miss you. If you do not return after two nights, I will come to Ramah."

She smiled, and I knew she understood what I meant. "Good," she whispered. "I don't want to be away from your bed any longer than tradition demands."

It seemed like only a few minutes before they were gone. I waved good-bye to them from the manor gates. I watched as they climbed the hill which would very quickly bypass the glen of my palm tree. I had hoped that just Deborah and I would be walking that road today. Instead, it was Deborah and Modan and twenty-seven of my men. I shrugged. Jealousy was an emotion I must not allow to possess me.

Indeed I had little time to think about Deborah. For that day and the next I was busy with household affairs. I met with my steward to review the condition of the estate. We were well into the dry season and the wheat harvest was almost complete. I toured some of the fields to be sure several rows of gleanings had been left for the poor to reap, according to the law of Moses.

I was particularly interested in the new method of farming called "terracing," which I had instituted last year. The hillsides were fertile but could produce only if landscaped in terraces. It worked well, and I was pleased to see that it almost doubled our wheat crop. We would need it, because next year was the Sabbatical Year, when Moses commanded us to allow the ground to lie fallow for a season. It was right and proper to honor Yahweh this way, but it would take preparation and an extra good harvest. I was glad we were having cool nights, even in this dry season. Cool nights meant heavy dew, which led to larger crops.

Because of the large number of kids, lambs, and calves born in the last few months, we needed to reassign duties of our shepherds and herdsman. Several young boys were given the responsibility of a flock and sent out seeking new pastures. I was concerned about the growing number of Caananite raiders in the area, and I discussed with my steward the possibility of enlarging our garrison of household guards. We decided to begin military training for several of our sturdy young men.

I toured the gardens to check on the vegetable crops. They would be good also. We had recovered well from the locust plague three years ago. New wells were sunk in various remote sections and boundary walls were set up to ensure a minimum of neighbor disputes.

Because we were doing so well on my estates, I decided that a sacrifice of thanksgiving to Yahweh was in order. I instructed the Levite who lived in our household to prepare a feast of thanksgiving and select several bullocks, rams, and goats for the sacrifice. They must be perfect specimens to fulfill the requirements of the law, and I asked him to begin immediately to search for the best.

The two days passed quickly, although Deborah was never far from my thoughts. I went to my lonely bed each night, tired from a busy day, but conscious of the coldness of my blankets without a wife to warm them. Strange. I had shared my bed with her only a few nights, yet it seemed she was an integral part of my life. I was glad when noon of the third day arrived, and I could begin to think about traveling to Ramah to be reunited with her.

Ramah was only a two-hour walk from

Bethel, or one hour for a young runner. Several times during those two days I had dispatched a runner to bring back news — and the news was good. Modan's mother was improving, and Deborah seemed to have brought stability and contentment, as well as some gaiety, to that household.

By midafternoon I was ready to go. The household was busy preparing for the Sabbath, which would begin at sundown, but Mother found time to speak to me.

"You're going to bring that girl back here, aren't you Beriah?" she demanded. Mother never requested; she always seemed to demand.

"Yes, Mother. It was her wish to live here with you."

Mother nodded, and it seemed to me her mouth had less of a pout than usual. "Good. Then I shall keep an eye on her. I will make her into a good wife for you, even if I have to take a switch to her."

I knew my mother well enough to know that she never took a switch to anybody. She didn't need to. The verbal lashings she constantly gave the servants — and family — were severe enough.

But I also knew Mother well enough to wonder about her desire to share her house with my bride. Was she attracted to her? Or was it just her need to dominate someone? That seemed more likely. A young girl, still a child, might be just the kind of person for her to exercise control over, like a domineering master over a slave, or a small boy over a dog. I wondered what this would do to Deborah's elfish spirit. I decided to keep an eye on this situation.

I said good-bye to Mother hastily and started out. I was alone, since most of the household guards had gone with Modan and Deborah. If I were assaulted by Canaanites, I would merely run. Not many Canaanites could run as fast as I. But no one was on the road, and I had a peaceful journey to Ramah.

I arrived at Ramah just before sundown. They were expecting me, of course. This was the beginning of the Sabbath. We would spend a quiet evening and day with the work laid aside until the following sundown, according the law of Moses.

Deborah met me in the courtyard, and she ran to me and put her arms around my neck. I was not accustomed to this kind of display of affection and wondered what Modan and his household would think of it. They only grinned, however, as though Deborah's actions were quite normal for the atmosphere she had created for their household.

As I held her in my arms, I heard her whisper in my ear, "I'm so glad you're here, Beriah. I've missed you."

I pressed her closely to me, feeling tears start in my eyes. "I have missed you too, my dear. You are indeed worth more than gold and silver."

She laughed, and her laugh was not at all mocking. It was . . . effervescent. Bubbling. Bursting forth from an elfin spirit of pure merriment. And infectious.

I grinned. "Modan," I called. "How is your mother?"

"Better. Your wife is a more skilled *rophe* than old Jehoaddah. The fever has gone, and soon she will be on her feet to resume her duties."

"Good. Is all ready for the Sabbath?"

"Yes. You have time to visit Mother before the shophar sounds."

We spent a very relaxing evening at Ramah, and Deborah and I retired early. Nothing in the law of Moses prevents sexual relations with one's wife during the Sabbath. This was wise, for only labor is forbidden. The begetting of sons is not a labor but an act of love, and a most appropriate way to spend a Sabbath night.

How strange and wonderful are the ways of Yahweh. He created his servants man and woman, created them in such a way that they too shall create. And the method he gave them to create is the most blissful and satisfying activity two human beings could indulge in. Deborah and I were discovering and exploring the secrets of creation.

8

We returned to Bethel on the first day of the week. Since we had left Ramah at sunrise, we arrived at our house in Bethel just as that household was beginning their work for the day. Fires had been rekindled and tasks were being assigned to the servants. We could hear Mother's shrill voice as we approached the house.

She turned from haranguing a servant and saw us coming in the gate. With a dismissing wave to the servant, she hurried across the courtyard to greet us.

"Well, it's about time you're here. These people you have given me for servants are of no value whatsoever. You should whip them all, Beriah. Every one of them. They're so stupid —"

"Mother, will you help Deborah arrange the master bedchamber for us? That's where we'll live for a while. I'm going to leave you two to discuss the shortcomings of the servants while I meet with my steward."

"That's right, Beriah. Go off and leave us,

just when I have so much to do. I wanted you to talk to that lazy Miriam, and to instruct that stupid Eshbaal about how to build a proper table, and to send old Zimri —"

Deborah's tinkling laugh stopped her. "Come on, Mother Zebiah, show me where our room is." She reached her hand to Mother's, saying, "I want to hear all about the servants. Maybe we can think of some way to make Miriam work harder, or Eshbaal to build a better table, and I want to hear all about old Zimri."

"Well. Old Zimri is a nuisance. He's so old. . . ."

I smiled as I watched the two women walk hand in hand toward the stairs leading to the upper chamber which would be our bedroom. Chattering. It would be interesting to see who would dominate whom.

Tola, my steward, kept me busy with affairs of the estate that day. One of my neighbors, Ashvath, a testy old Ephraimite of the Zabadite clan, insisted that a certain water hole was on his property. He had posted his household guards there to keep our shepherds away. I went to his house and spent several hours with him, cajoling, flattering, offering understanding. In the end I agreed that the water hole was indeed his, but since it was in a valley between two of our larger pastures, our flocks needed to water there as we traveled back and forth. I reminded Ashvath of the well in the pasture near Mizpah which we shared, even though it was on my property. He grudgingly agreed to a truce. Then I invited him to visit us to meet my bride.

"I heard you married a little child," he grumbled. "Sorry I couldn't come to your wedding."

"You'll like Deborah. She's very cheerful. She and Tirzah should become friends."

Ashvath's daughter Tirzah was the same age as Deborah. Perhaps he was jealous because I hadn't taken her as my wife. He wasn't as wealthy as Becher, and my father's choice was understandable. Nevertheless I'm sure it rankled the old man.

My steward must have presented me with seventy-seven similar problems that day. Many of them were related to the flocks and herds — what rams should be bred with which ewes, the north pasture was infested with snakes, the new shepherd was too young and inexperienced to handle a flock alone, and a strange disease was spreading among the goats in the south pasture. I dealt with each trouble as briefly as I could, because always there was another problem waiting for me somewhere else.

Some of the problems arose because of disputes among the servants. Abihud and Shephuphan had been fighting because Abihud's goats were invading Shephuphan's sheep pasture and hogging the water. Misham and Shemed both claimed Ishpah's daughter for their sons' betrothal. Pispa had contracted a disease because he visited a Canaanite prostitute in Anathoth.

I had little patience with these disputes involving human stupidity. Sometimes people can be more childish than animals. Nevertheless, I dealt with them as best I could, although many of my solutions were inadequate.

At last the long tiring day was over, and the sun sank toward the western hills. With my steward Tola, I was on my way toward the house in Bethel. We were both exhausted. We had walked about twenty miles that day, journeying from one side of my estates to another, but the physical exertion did not tire me as much as the mental labor. Solving human problems is exhausting.

We had come within sight of the manor house where I lived, the friendly white walls gleaming in the late afternoon sunshine. It would be good to be home, to relax at a table of good food, to spend a quiet evening with my family. With Deborah. She had made all the difference in the world to my lonely life.

Then I noticed, far to the south, a group of armed men coming out of the trees and down the road from Ramah. I counted six of them.

I grasped Tola's arm and pointed. "Look there," I said. "What do you make of that?"

The steward was considerably older than I, and the day's travels had exhausted him. He wiped the sweat from his forehead and tried to focus on where I pointed.

"Canaanites," he muttered. "We'd better hurry."

We could easily run to the gates of my house before they arrived. I was concerned about Tola, however; even that small run would be difficult for him.

"No," I said. "Not Canaanites. Israelites."

Tola breathed a sigh of relief. I think his main concern was having to run the few hundred paces to the gates.

What were they doing here? They were armed. Spears and swords. One of them carried a bow and a quiver of arrows.

We plodded on toward the gates, watching their approach. I sent Tola inside to alert the household that we might be having guests tonight. Then I stood just outside the gates waiting for them.

Their leader was a tall man with a short

curly gray beard. Middle-aged, but strong and wiry. He carried a spear and sword. Heavy brows topped eyes that seemed sullen and angry.

I held up my hand in a greeting of friendship.

"Yahweh bless you, strangers. You have come far. Stay with me tonight. Enjoy my hospitality. You are welcome here."

The leader raised his hand. "Greetings in the name of Yahweh, to Beriah ben Jonathan of Ephraim. I accept your kind offer of hospitality. I am Ophrah ben Meonothai, from Debir."

Everyone in Israel knew Ophrah ben Meonothai. He was grandson of the famous Othniel, conqueror of Debir, deliverer of Israel from the Syrian invasion, and first judge of Israel.

"I am honored," I said, "to have a distinguished son of Judah in my home. Please come in."

Inside the gates, I was pleased to see that preparations for entertaining guests were already under way. I led them to an upper chamber where we did most of our entertaining.

"Please be seated, my friends." I motioned toward the benches against the wall. The long table before them was bare now, but soon would be laden with food and drink.

"Ah, here is my wife Deborah to tend to your needs."

I caught my breath. Deborah was wearing a blue gown belted high at the waist. Her fresh youthful face seemed to shine. Her hair gleamed with oil. She had had no warning of visitors. Could she have prepared herself so carefully for my return?

She carried a bowl of water and towel. As soon as Ophrah seated himself on a bench, she knelt to wash his feet. In doing so, she gave him a shy smile. I could tell Ophrah was charmed by her.

Before my marriage, Mother had performed these duties. At times her sharp tongue had embarrassed me, as she had my father in years past. Now, it seemed, the chores had been wisely divided — Mother supervised the cooking of the evening meal, and Deborah tended the needs of our guests.

A servant entered with a tray containing a pitcher of wine and several cups. He placed it on the table and began to serve our guests.

As the cup of wine was placed in Ophrah's hands, I spoke the formal words of welcome.

"Welcome to my house, friend. You may stay for two nights and the day between. My house is yours. My wealth is yours. My servants are yours. I myself am at your service."

"Thank you, Beriah. You are kind. But we shall not stay more than just one night. We'll leave tomorrow morning."

"As you wish, Ophrah. Perhaps we will have the opportunity to entertain you again on your return journey."

I could say this without appearing inquisitive. To ask a guest where he was going and what his business was would be insulting. But I knew he would probably return through Bethel on his way to Debir in the territory of Judah, so my offer was neither discourteous nor meddlesome.

However, he chose to speak freely of the reason for his journey. "I go to Shechem," he said. "I have sworn an oath. I am the avenger of blood."

"I see," I said politely, although I didn't see. I hoped he would continue, but it would be rude to press him.

Everyone knew Shechem was a city of refuge. The Levites who lived there were well-known for their protection of refugees. The law of Moses said that a man fleeing from an avenger of blood could seek asylum in one of six cities and be sheltered from the blood revenge.

One of the cities of refuge was Hebron, only a few miles from Debir. I wondered if he would tell me why the person fleeing his vengeance would go all the way to Shechem, but I hesitated to ask lest I appear discourteous. Perhaps after the food was served and he had drunk several more cups of wine, Ophrah would tell me more. But he seemed to burn with a desire to talk about his problem.

"The man I seek," he said slowly, "is Bethgader ben Hareph. He murdered my son."

I had never heard of this man. But I knew the law of Moses. Ophrah had every right to do what he was doing.

"Do you think the Levites at Shechem will surrender him?" I asked.

"I don't know. I have heard different rumors about the Shechem Levites. Some say they are scrupulously honest and will hold a fair trial. Others say they are open to bribes. Do you know anything about them?"

"No."

I glanced at Deborah, who had by now washed the feet of all six of the Judahites. She picked up her basin and towel and came to me.

She would probably know. Her father had many dealings with the Levites in Shechem, and the asylum offered to fugitives would be something often discussed in their family. But it was not proper to include a woman in a conversation such as this. This was man's business. Women belonged in the kitchen, or bedroom, or at best kneeling before a man to wash his feet, as she did now.

Nevertheless, Deborah was wise and discreet. She would not push herself forward more than a woman should in a man's discussion.

I decided to bring her into the conversation. "My wife Deborah comes from Shechem," I said. "Perhaps she would know the disposition of the Levites there."

Ophrah smiled. "Your wife is a lovely young lady. I would be glad to hear her opinion about the Levites of Shechem."

Deborah had finished her ministrations to my feet, and sat back on her heels. She now looked up shyly. "I know the Levites there," she said quietly. "The chief Levite, Meraioth ben Zerahiah, has been in our home often. He is a good, honest man. He will give Bethgader a fair hearing."

Deborah looked directly at Ophrah. "If you offer him a bribe, sir, it would only insult him."

Had she gone beyond the bounds of proper decorum for a wife? To answer when spoken to was good; to add an uninvited comment, which bordered on reproving our guest, was indecent.

"Thank you, Deborah." Ophrah's harsh features had softened and he spoke gently. "I will follow your advice. I'm sure this Levite will turn over the refugee to me for my blood vengeance."

"If your cause is just, sir." Deborah's soft voice sounded loud in that suddenly quiet room.

I frowned. Should I say something now? A sharp word of reproof to a wife who had gone too far? But her attitude was meek and submissive. I found it difficult to be angry with her. I glanced at Ophrah, expecting him to be insulted.

But he leaned forward, seemingly willing to speak to the woman kneeling before me.

"My cause is just, my dear." His voice was gentle. "My son Merari was betrothed to a daughter of my neighbor. Beth-gader claimed he had been promised the girl by a previous betrothal. They fought, and Beth-gader killed my son. I have sworn before Yahweh that Merari's blood is on my hands, and I will be his avenger."

Deborah's keen eyes looked boldly at Ophrah. "And that is why Beth-gader fled to Shechem? Because you claim the right of blood vengeance?"

"Of course, my dear."

"Please, sir." Deborah's voice, which had been soft, became even softer, and we had to strain to hear her. "It seems to me the fault was not with these two boys, but with their parents, if both entered into a betrothal contract for the same woman."

In the few seconds of silence which followed her quiet statement, I sensed that no one breathed. Certainly not I. I began to feel my cheeks burning with embarrassment. Not only had she insulted our guest, but she — a woman — had just reproved a man. And she wasn't even a woman, but a . . . a girl. A child.

I opened my mouth to say something. But what could I say? Deborah's words were insulting, but her manner, her demeanor, was shy and submissive. I glanced at Ophrah.

He was running his fingers through his grizzled beard. The frown on his forehead might have been anger — or thoughtfulness. I could not tell which.

He pursed his lips. "Beriah," he said slowly not taking his eyes off Deborah, "you have a truly amazing wife."

"Er . . . Ophrah —" I wanted to apologize but I couldn't find the words. I wasn't even sure if he were offended. I bit my lip and remained silent.

"Please, sir." Deborah's soft voice was as far from being insulting as anything could possibly be. "When you speak to Maráioth the Levite, I know you will respect his judgment. He is a wise man."

"I will, Deborah." Ophrah leaned back. "Thank you."

She nodded, then picked up her basin and towel and left the room.

I wasn't sure whether to struggle with an apology or not.

Before I could say anything, Ophrah turned to me and said, "What she said was so obvious, I don't know why none of us ever thought of it before. Those boys weren't at fault. The fault lies with Hareph and myself. We both made betrothal commitments for our sons. And the girls' father, too, must share the blame. He had no right. . . ."

His voice trailed off. What should I say? Actually, I felt embarrassed, that my wife — a child — had made the whole matter clear to him. Meanwhile I — who should have been the wise host — had nothing intelligent to contribute to the discussion. I was made to look a fool.

I felt I must say something, to at least redeem myself as a man of wisdom. "Have you considered going to Shamgar for a judgment?" I asked.

"Bah! Shamgar is as stupid as his ox goad."

If the rumors about Israel's present *shaphat* proved to be only half true, what Ophrah said would be accurate. People whispered that his judgments were stupid. He was honest enough, not susceptible to bribes, but if two people stated their cases before him, he would respond favorably to the one who could present the best case emotionally. He had no wisdom or insight into human nature.

"You're right," I said, hoping to appear intelligent in his eyes. "What Israel needs is a *shaphat* raised by Yahweh himself."

"Right!" Ophrah's fervor showed how deeply he felt about it. "Just because a man claims to have killed five hundred Canaanites all by himself does not mean Yahweh has given him wisdom to judge Israel."

"Tell me, Ophrah, do you know anyone in Israel who is wise enough to do that? Someone like your ancestor Othniel."

He chuckled. "Othniel. Yes. Let me tell you something about Othniel that is not in the Sacred Story."

I leaned forward eagerly. The Sacred Story told the history of Israel from the beginning of creation. We all knew it by heart, having heard it recited by our elders all our lives.

"Othniel's wisdom," he continued, "has reached legendary proportions. But what the Sacred Story does not say — and this was told to me as a child by my father Meonothai — is this. A large part of Othniel's wisdom came from his wife, Achsah."

"Really?" I stared at him. "If this is true, then why isn't it in the Sacred Story?"

Ophrah grunted and ran his fingers through his beard. "Because Achsah wanted it that way. She felt men might hesitate to accept Othniel's judgments if they knew a woman were advising him."

I frowned. Could this be? How would I feel if I knew that one of Israel's shaphats depended on a woman for a large part of his wisdom? Evidently a lot of Israelite men had felt the same; they had not wanted their great hero to be controlled by a woman's intelligence.

Ophrah continued. "In my family, we have often discussed what would have happened had Achsah openly declared herself as a shaphat of Israel, appointed by Yahweh himself, equal to her husband Othniel. Would the people have come to her for judgments?"

I shook my head. "I doubt it. Who would want a woman judging them?"

Ophrah leaned back in his seat. "*I* would.

Right now, I'd gladly submit to anyone appointed by Yahweh — male or female — with more wisdom than Shamgar. Why, even your young wife has more wisdom than he!"

I studied the face of the man before me. It was lined with suffering and experience, reflecting wisdom gained by many years. He had listened to Deborah and even to me. This showed he would thoughtfully consider advice from anyone younger than himself — even a woman. Did he reflect a new trend of thinking in Israel? Or did the tradition prevail that men, and only men, were God's true creation, and women were their helpmates?

I would like to have raised this question with him. But at that moment my mother and several servants came into the room, carrying food which they placed before our guests. A kid had been roasted, its savory odors making us even hungrier. Bread, vegetables, and fruit were spread out on the table. The men began to eat ravenously. Soon the atmosphere of the room changed from serious contemplation of their mission to one of relaxation and conviviality. Wine cups were refilled.

I looked at Mother, who was busy watching the servants with a critical eye. Had she been in this room a few moments earlier, would she have remained silent? As shrewish as Mother was, she might have spoken her opinion on the superiority of men and the inferiority of women — but in a strident, derisive tone of voice.

Then Deborah came in with a fresh pitcher of wine, and began to quietly fill the fast-emptying cups. She would not have interrupted our discussion, of course. She was much too shy.

But what if Ophrah had asked her opinion about the place of women in society? What would she have said? I decided to ask her some time. Some time later, when we were alone. Some time when I would have an opportunity to straighten out her thinking.

She was so young. She needed my wisdom as an older, more experienced man — yes, a man — to make sure she didn't fall into the pitfall of thinking of herself as better than she really was. Yes, I would talk to her.

Later. For now, I must entertain my guests.

9

Ophrah and his men left the next morning as they had planned. Just before they went, Deborah gave Ophrah a sack containing bread and cheese for their journey.

"You are very kind," Ophrah said to her. "And wise. I shall follow your advice, seek out Maráioth the Levite at Shechem, and submit to his wisdom on this matter."

Deborah smiled, and I could tell Ophrah was charmed by her. She said, "Please stop by my father's home. He will be pleased to offer you his hospitality."

"I will."

"And tell him that all is well with me, that I am content in my new life with Beriah."

Ophrah nodded. "And I shall add my own observations on the charm and wisdom of his daughter."

As the host, I offered the traditional words of farewell. "Yahweh go with you," I said. "May he lift up his countenance upon you, and give you a safe journey."

"Thank you, Beriah. You have been a gracious host. I shall always count you as a friend." He glanced at Deborah before adding, "And I shall not soon forget your lovely wife."

With a final wave, he was gone. We watched as Ophrah and his men climbed the trail toward the north which would take them to Shechem. A trail I had followed just two weeks ago, on my way to claim my bride. With my half-brother Rakem.

I must plan my blood revenge. Heber the Kenite was secure in his home near Kedesh. He was probably gloating about how he killed the brother of the rich Israelite Beriah. He wouldn't get away with it. I didn't know yet how I would do it, but I would. And I must begin to plan today.

Perhaps I should go to Modan, Rakem's son, and include him in my revenge. But not yet. I must have a plan first. I must somehow work out a scheme to lure Heber out of his home territory. I must not meet him in single combat. There must be some other way. . . .

With these thoughts swirling in my mind, I was startled by a soft hand on my arm.

"What is it Beriah?" Deborah's anxious face looked up into mine. "You seem so unhappy just now. Surely Ophrah's leaving didn't sadden you. What evil thought brought such a deep frown to your forehead?"

I closed my hand over hers and shook my head. "Nothing to concern you, my dear. You're right. I should not be so somber today."

As I looked into her youthful face, I suddenly wanted to do something far different from planning my brother's revenge. I wanted to spend the day with her, to be cheerful and carefree, to enjoy her company and listen to her sing.

"Today," I said, "let's go to my palm tree. You'll love the place. I can tell you the words to my new poem, and maybe you can find a tune for it."

She greeted this suggestion with wide eyes and broad smile. "Oh, can we, Beriah? But . . . a palm tree? Where is that? Surely not up here in the mountains?"

I laughed. "Yes, up here in the mountains. My own special palm tree, where I spend many hours composing empty poems and wishing I had someone who could sing them for me."

She clapped her hands and grinned. "I know just the person who would love to do that. Let me get my lyre."

She turned and ran toward our bedchamber. I gave orders to one of the servants to prepare some bread and cheese and a flask of wine. I discussed with my steward Tola a few tasks he could do today in my absence.

Then I spoke to one of the young men. "Stand up there today," I told him, pointing to a platform on the southwest corner of the wall. "Deborah and I will be at my palm tree. Watch the roads around. If you see any Canaanites who might be hostile, round up a few men and come running out to defend us."

He nodded and went to the wall to take his station. He would watch us as we walked the half mile to the glen. Then he would lose sight of us as we entered the copse of pine trees which sheltered the hollow where Deborah and I would spend at least a part of this day. We would be observed and protected but still have some privacy.

Deborah came with her lyre. The servant brought the refreshments.

And Mother came. "That's right, Beriah. Go off and play and leave me here with these lazy servants. You know how much I have to do today. And you won't even leave Deborah here to help me. You don't seem to care —"

"Mother, we'll just be gone a few hours, and we'll only be a short distance. This afternoon —"

"By this afternoon, this place could be in shambles. You don't know how lazy that

Miriam is, and old Zimri —"

Deborah's hand touched Mother's arm. "You are so good at managing the servants, Mother Zebiah. I have seen that in just the few days I've been here. You're the only one I know who can get as much work out of Miriam as you do. And you have such patience with old Zimri. When I return this afternoon, I'll sing a song for you. Maybe Beriah's song, if he'll let me."

I laughed. "Of course I will, my dear. Now come on. You'll be just fine, Mother."

At the gate I glanced back. Mother had already turned toward the house. I could hear her voice scolding someone — Miriam or Zimri or anybody else in reach of her shrill tongue. I could hardly wait to find the comfort and peace of my palm tree.

As I expected, Deborah was delighted with the glen. She clapped her hands and exclaimed, "It's lovely, Beriah! Who would have thought to find a palm tree in a place like this? And this carpet . . . and the fragrance of pines, and that spring — is it cool here all day?"

"All day. And there's a lark living up there in that pine tree who sings so sweetly, you won't believe it!"

"Oh, I believe it! This place must be what Eden looked like!"

We sat on the stone bench, and I taught her the words to my empty poem. It was not empty long. She strummed her lyre and hummed while I recited it. Almost immediately she tried phrases matched to tunes. My poem came alive. Never had a verse of mine sounded so good.

Until now, I had thought there was no sweeter sound than the lark in the pine tree. But I had discovered someone whose voice was sweeter.

We worked on the song all morning. When at last we were both satisfied, she plucked the strings and sang the final version.

Sing praises to Yahweh, O my soul.
Sing praises to him on the highest mountain.
Sing praises to him in the deepest valley.
Sing praises to him beside the still waters.
O my soul, sing praises to Yahweh,
  for he is good,
  his love endures forever.

There was more, of course; much more. The song had several verses. She had helped me revise some of the phrasing so the final product seemed to me the best I had ever done. As a husband-and-wife team, we were superb.

"Let's sing it for your mother," she said.

"Maybe she'll forget about old Zimri and lazy Miriam for a while."

"Too bad we didn't have this last night. You could have sung it for our visitors."

She sighed. "Poor Ophrah. He's such a troubled man. I do hope Maráioth the Levite gives him good advice. That's too heavy a burden for any man to carry."

"But — he's a blood avenger. He's sworn an oath. He has to carry that burden. It's the law."

She looked up at me as we sat together on the bench. The look I saw in her eyes was troubled. A tear formed in one of them.

"Oh . . . Beriah. Beriah. Ophrah isn't the only one who carries a horrible burden."

I frowned, knowing what she meant.

"Surely you don't mean I should cast that 'horrible burden' aside, forsake the law, forswear myself, and let poor Rakem go unavenged?"

She lowered her eyes. Perhaps my words had been too stern. I softened them.

"My dear, no harm will come to me. I promise you I will not face Heber the Kenite in battle. I'm not that foolish."

"But —" Now her words were spoken so softly I had to bend my head to hear them. "But you *will* take your revenge, won't you?"

I nodded. Her head was bowed and she

didn't notice. But my silence spoke more eloquently than my nod.

"Beriah, my love." There was a slight catch in her voice. "What if . . . what if you do somehow take Heber's life. Will that be the end of it? Or will someone in Heber's family, maybe one of his sons, take the vow of a blood avenger and come after you?"

I shrugged. "If that happens, then so be it. Yahweh's will be done."

"Yahweh's will!" She looked up, and her voice trembled. "What a strange thing for Yahweh to will. To kill. To avenge. To shed blood. To never forgive. To —"

"But it's the law!" How could I explain this to a young child? "We live and die by the law of Moses. We are Israelites! We must obey the law."

"Israelites obey God. The purpose of the law of Moses is to help us know what is Yahweh's will."

At the time she said it, I did not recognize the profundity of her statement. Only later, as I reflected on this conversation, did I realize such an observation was much too intelligent for a fourteen-year-old child — a girl child at that.

But at the time, I was thinking only of an answer to her. "And how can we know the will of Yahweh unless we go by the law?"

Deborah was looking up at me, and her eyes were soft and trusting. She reached for my hand. Then she spoke, softly and shyly. "We need someone to interpret the law for us. Someone wise. Someone not blinded by his own emotions and prejudices."

"We don't have such a person. Certainly not Shamgar." I recalled Ophrah's phrase. "Shamgar is as stupid as his ox goad."

She smiled. I was filled with a sense of superiority. She appreciated my wit as well as my wisdom.

Again she spoke softly. "But Maráioth the Levite is not. I hope Ophrah finds the wisdom he needs right now. He is so filled with hate and sorrow and loneliness and . . . such a blind devotion to the letter of the law. . . ."

Her voice trailed off and we sat there in silence. She leaned her head on my shoulder and I put my arm around her. I recalled Ophrah's words about my wife's wisdom and clarity of thinking. He had listened to her, accepted her mild reproof, and followed her advice.

She had been talking just now about Ophrah's problem. His hate. His emotions which clouded his thinking. His — what were her words? — *blind devotion to the letter of the law.* Ophrah's problem.

Or was she really talking about mine?

Suddenly, above and behind us, the lark burst into song, filling the silence of the glen with music. We listened quietly for a while. It seemed to me the lark's melody was not nearly as lovely as my wife's singing when she sang the song we wrote together.

Was that because we wrote it together? Was it because it was a joint effort, and the one I loved made it into such a beautiful anthem of praise to Yahweh? Was it my love for her which made me think of her as more beautiful than any bird in the tree?

I gripped her shoulder more tightly, and it seemed to me she responded. Soon we would have to go back to the house, to Mother, to her shrill voice, to the mundane problems of lazy Miriam and old Zimri. But not yet.

We sat quietly, listening to the song of our lark. Under our palm tree. Enjoying the moment. Sharing our love.

Our palm tree. No longer Beriah's palm tree. We could look forward to many more of these brief sojourns into our garden of Eden in the future.

10

In the weeks that followed, I became aware of several subtle changes in my household.

Mother's tongue seemed to lose a bit of its acidity. She showed more patience with the servants and even smiled occasionally. Deborah continued to praise her for her efficiency, her ability to handle servants, and her management skills. Mother responded by trying to live up to that praise.

This led to a relaxation among the servants. Miriam worked harder. Whether this was because Mother was not as harsh with her, or because she was trying to please Deborah, I could not tell. Old Zimri hummed some of Deborah's tunes as he shuffled around the house doing his inconsequential chores.

Home became a very pleasant place after a long day in the fields. All the cares of my vast estate seemed to slip away as I sat with Mother and Deborah in the quiet evenings. My wife often played her lyre and sang for us. During those times, I noticed that the servants gathered in a small group nearby to listen.

Deborah and I made many trips to our palm tree, where we composed new songs. One in particular which I recall reflected our family happiness.

Blessed is the man whose faith is secure,
    whose trust is the peace of Yahweh.
His wife gives him respect;
    his children rise up and praise him.
His neighbors give him honor and admiration;
    behold, a good word is on their lips.
For he gives Yahweh his allegiance,
    and Israel is secure because of his wisdom.

At the time I composed this poem, I thought the words were mine. But looking back, I realize they were a joint effort. Deborah made subtle suggestions as I framed the words. Then she put them to music.

We sang this song to Mother, and it brought tears to her eyes. Her face softened, reflecting the beauty which lay beneath the harshness. We were sitting on the rooftop enjoying the evening breeze, watching the sun fade into the western hills. I looked over the balcony into the courtyard; the servants had gathered there to listen.

What more could a man ask for in this

life? Only one thing: children. Children to "rise up and praise him," as our song said. But they would come. Deborah and I were young. And Yahweh was good.

Ophrah returned from Shechem, and we welcomed him once again. This time he was in no hurry, and accepted my invitation to stay with us for the traditional length of a visit: two nights and the day between.

"Beriah," he said to me, "I want to tell you about my experience at Shechem."

I had hoped he would. He had not broached the subject on the evening he arrived, but now, in the early morning as we sat in the courtyard in the shade of the house, he seemed inclined to talk.

The sun had risen less than an hour ago. Around us the household went about their work quietly. Deborah and Mother had thoughtfully assigned the servants tasks which would not be noisy and active, so we could talk. Deborah was supervising a group of servants in the corner of the yard where the outdoor cooking was done. They had killed a young ram today and would be roasting it for this evening's feast.

"I am very much interested, my friend," I replied. "And did you find Maráioth the Levite as wise as Deborah said he would be?"

Ophrah nodded. "Why don't you ask your

wife to join us in our discussion? I think she would be interested in what Maráioth had to say."

This surprised me. Seldom did a man suggest that a woman be included in the discussion. I did, however, know that Deborah had charmed this man. He was not the sort of person I should be jealous of. His grizzled beard and lined face suggested he could be the age of Deborah's father. Or my father, for that matter.

I called to Deborah, who turned to look my way. When I asked her to come join our discussion, she smiled. After leaving a few last-minute instructions with the servants, she came toward us.

Ophrah stood and arranged a bench for her. "Please sit down, my dear. I'm sure you would like to hear about my conversation with Maráioth the Levite at Shechem."

Deborah smiled and clapped her hands, like a child who has just been given a new toy. "Oh yes! I'd love to! Thank you so much for being thoughtful enough to tell me. You are surely aware of my concern for you and your mission to Shechem."

Her actions and tone of voice were that of a child, but her words contained the maturity of a wise old lady. I was aware of Ophrah's reaction. He seemed more animated, more pleased at the prospect of sharing our discussion with her.

"Deborah, you were perfectly right about Maráioth. He is a wise man, whose judgment I respect."

"I'm glad," said Deborah.

It seemed to me that the discussion was between Ophrah and Deborah. I was omitted. I felt like one of the servants eavesdropping on one of our family sessions when Deborah sang.

"Maráioth listened to me," continued Ophrah, "and seemed to understand my point of view. But he had also listened to Beth-gader. He said he had very carefully considered the case, and felt qualified to render a judgment."

"That Beth-gader could stay," said Deborah.

Ophrah glanced at her sharply. "Yes. How did you know?"

She smiled. "It's the only sensible judgment he could render in this case."

"Er . . . yes, I suppose so."

Maráioth's decision meant that Beth-gader was only guilty of manslaughter, not malicious murder. Had Maráioth rendered the other verdict, the youth would have been delivered to Ophrah for the blood revenge.

"And how is Maráioth's health?"

When Deborah asked this question, I raised my eyebrows. Why would she ask that now? What did that have to do with this discussion? I could tell by Ophrah's questioning look that he wondered too.

"He's well." Then Ophrah opened his eyes wide. "Ah . . . yes. I see. Beriah, your wife is well versed in the law of Moses."

Then I too understood why Deborah had asked about Maráioth's health. The law of Moses stated that the fugitive, if his cause were just, could stay in the city of refuge until the death of the chief priest there. The chief priest's death would then atone for Beth-gader's blood guilt.

"Poor Beth-gader." Deborah shook her head slowly. "He's facing a long, cruel punishment. Exile. Cut off from his home and family for as long as Maráioth lives. How sad."

"But my dear," said Ophrah. "Isn't that justice? He *is* a murderer."

"He killed your son, yes. But in a fair fight. And the cause of their dispute was the stupidity of the three fathers involved, who made betrothal arrangements which were illegal and greedy."

Both Ophrah and I gasped. What was she saying? She was insulting Ophrah to his face. Calling him stupid. And greedy. And accusing him of doing something illegal. This was a serious act of rudeness.

Ophrah's face began to turn red. How deeply was he insulted and hurt by Deborah's thoughtless statement?

Then Deborah reached out and took Ophrah's hand in hers. She spoke softly and with obvious sincerity. "Please, Father Ophrah. Forgive me for speaking to you like this. I don't mean to be insulting. I only want you to know the truth."

Something about Deborah's demeanor — her humility, her sincerity, her deep concern for Ophrah — must have communicated itself to our guest.

His other hand closed over hers. "Yes, my dear," he said softly. "I understand. And I suppose . . . I suppose you're right. The guilt is as much mine as Beth-gader's."

She smiled. "You are truly a big man to admit that. I admire you so much. I think you could even go to the boy's father when you return to Debir, and make your peace with him."

I sat on the bench staring openmouthed at my wife. She looked so young, so innocent, so childish! And yet what she was saying to Ophrah contained wisdom far beyond her years.

"But my dear," said Ophrah, "what about

my blood revenge against Beth-gader? I have sworn a vow. . . ."

"Beth-gader's guilt has been assumed by Maráioth the Levite," she replied. "That releases you from your burden. Now you can live in peace, if you speak to the boy's father."

"Yes," he said. Then he sighed. "Yes. My burden. You are so right. Thank you."

"When your burden is lifted," said Deborah softly, "then maybe Beth-gader could return to his home."

"What!" Ophrah seemed to shrink back a little, even while holding Deborah's hand. "I don't know about that. I have sworn an oath —"

Deborah smiled, and I could see the pressure she put on the gnarled hands she held. "Please think about it, Father Ophrah. Now please excuse me. I must get back to my household duties."

She rose from the bench, Ophrah rising with her. Slowly he released her hands. "Thank you, my dear," he murmured as she turned to walk away. His gaze followed her as she walked across the courtyard toward the cooking ovens.

At this point, I examined my own emotions. I was neither jealous nor resentful, but at the same time in awe of my wife's cleverness. Deborah had somehow turned an insult into wise counsel. She had expressed a love for him which caused me no jealousy whatsoever. It left me breathless.

Ophrah shook his head. "Beriah, you have a truly remarkable wife." His voice, though soft, was fervent.

"I'm a little astonished myself," I replied. "She continues to amaze me."

"Do you recall our discussion several nights ago, when we both wished God would raise up a shaphat in Israel who had true wisdom and insight?"

"Yes."

"Is it possible. . . ."

I gasped. "No! Of course not! What you are suggesting is *not* possible! Why — she's a woman — only a child!"

"But the wisdom of Yahweh is upon her. She's —"

"No, Ophrah! No! She's my wife! I'll not have it!"

He looked at me steadily, noting I'm sure the rising color in my face, which I myself could feel. He sighed.

"As you wish, my friend."

A silence stretched out between us. His tongue was stilled by courtesy. Mine with rage. Had he not been a guest in my home, I would have turned my back on him and walked away. As it was, I was barely civil to him. My coldness lasted throughout the day.

When I bade farewell to him and his men the next morning, it was with formality and no warmth. I watched as they walked up the hill following the trail toward the south. Past our palm tree.

Perhaps I should go to the palm tree. Now. Alone. To try to think about this. To make some decisions. Reach some understandings . . . about my wife. Perhaps talk to her.

But I could not. There was that dispute over the north border with Ashvath which I had postponed one day too long as it was. And the reports of vandals in the fields east of Bethel. And those ewes in Timor's flock. . . .

There was too much to be done. I would deal with my wife later.

11

The affairs of my estate kept me so busy I did not have a chance to talk with Deborah about her conduct with Ophrah. Perhaps it was just as well. Let it die down. Forget it. Allow her to assume the role of wife — and, I hoped, mother.

The first part of Deborah's obligation — wife — she fulfilled admirably. I enjoyed returning home in the late afternoons and being with her. Mother was pleasant company also these days. The entire household developed a congenial and cheerful atmosphere. Laughter was heard often, especially from the servants. Before Deborah's coming, they had been a somber group.

My present situation was the way I wanted it. This was the way a man of Israel should live. A benevolent God planned it that way when he created first the man, then the woman from the man's side. The woman was his helpmate, who should serve him and make his life more comfortable. Then he could do the tasks the wise deity had assigned him in this world. Deborah was fulfilling her role; now I could better fulfill mine.

Only one thing was missing from this household of perfection: children. Children came from God, and for some reason, he withheld them from us. The months slipped by; still there was no sign of new life in Deborah's womb. We were certainly doing our part; our lovemaking was sweet and satisfying. Once again I marveled at the wisdom and goodness of our Creator, who made us in such a way that the procreation of mankind would not only be efficient but ecstatic.

Nevertheless, it produced no results.

When a whole year had passed, and no son and heir had been born, I began to wonder. Why was Yahweh withholding his creative hand?

At least Deborah had not tried to assume any pretense of being Israel's new shaphat. I concluded that this idea was only Ophrah's dreams, fostered by his personal family history. His grandmother Achsah had been a wise adviser to her husband, Othniel, Israel's first judge. Nobody else would conceive such a preposterous idea. Certainly not Deborah.

As the months slid by in this idyllic setting, my vow of blood revenge faded. I did not completely forget it; I merely shoved it to the back of my mind. Those few times I recalled it, I told myself it was a lifetime vow, and I was young. Not now. Later. When the time was ripe.

A full year had passed since my marriage when a runner arrived from Ramah, from the household of my nephew Modan. Breathlessly he told us of a visitor from the south who had arrived just a few hours ago, wounded and exhausted, at the gates of my house in Ramah. He had been set upon by a roving band of Canaanites, his servants either killed or driven off. He himself was beaten, robbed, and left for dead.

"Sir," gasped the messenger, "Modan respectfully requests that you come in person. The visitor wants to speak with you. And Deborah. He specifically asked for Deborah."

"Deborah?" I frowned. Why? Perhaps his wounds were serious, and he had heard from Modan of Deborah's skill as a healer. If that were the case, then she must come, of course. I could not refuse a traveler whatever assistance I had to offer.

Within the hour, Deborah and I set out for Ramah, accompanied by twelve armed guards. The Canaanites had grown bolder during the past year, and armed bands roamed the highways seeking unguarded victims. Some in Israel were wondering if King Jabin of Hazor had been openly encouraging these attacks.

Modan met us at the gates of my house in Ramah and led us immediately to the upper room where his guest lay on a pallet on the floor.

"Greetings, friend." I knelt beside him. "Welcome to my home. Stay as long as you need to heal your wounds. My house is yours. My servants are at your command. My wealth is yours. My —"

"Please, Beriah." The man's voice was urgent as he interrupted my ritual greeting. "I need your help."

I looked closely at the man on the bed. His lean face was wrinkled with age, and by his gray beard and hair I judged he was older, past middle age. An Israelite. And in need of help.

"You shall have my help, friend. Now, tell me your name."

The man sat up. He was obviously not seriously injured.

"I am Hareph ben Hur of Judah."

The name was vaguely familiar. I knew I had heard it before, but I couldn't place it. Then I heard a gasp from Deborah, who stood just behind me.

"Please, sir," she said shyly. "Are you the father of Beth-gader?"

"Yes, my dear. And you must be Deborah."

I recalled then where I had heard of Hareph. Ophrah had mentioned him. But only my wife had remembered that he was the father of the boy who had slain Ophrah's son. But how would he know Deborah? Perhaps Modan had told him. Yes. Modan had mentioned Deborah as one who could heal his wounds. Yet he didn't seem to be badly wounded.

"Please, help me stand up," said Hareph.

Deborah and I helped him stand. He seemed well enough. A few bruises on his face, a little stiffness in his joints. But not seriously ill or injured.

Modan brought him some wine, and he sat on a bench to drink it. Then he began his story. "I'm on my way to Shechem," he said, "to find my son. I hope I can bring him home."

"Is that wise, my friend?" I too sat on a bench and accepted a cup of wine from Modan. "I believe Ophrah has sworn a vow before Yahweh of blood revenge."

Hareph nodded. "Ophrah came to me several months ago. We talked about what had happened. He told me what Deborah had said, and of her wisdom. We both realized that the two boys were not at fault. We were. We should never have allowed that thieving Shobal to betroth his daughter to two young men at the same time."

"But — you didn't know."

"True enough. When we found out, we were angry. We should have foreseen that our sons would be angry too. And being young, they settled it between them in the way young men do."

"And one was killed. Ophrah's son."

"Yes." Hareph turned and looked at Deborah, who stood near the door listening intently. "Deborah, my dear. Please come over here and sit beside me. I want to ask you something."

This was a man's discussion, but I could not refuse his request. As a guest in my home, that was his right. Deborah came quietly and sat on the bench beside him. He reached out and took her hand, reminding me of the way Ophrah had treated her last year. A fatherly gesture.

"Ophrah told me about you. He said Yahweh has given you wisdom."

"Ophrah exaggerates." Deborah lowered her eyes. "I . . . I really didn't —"

"According to my friend Ophrah, your wisdom was responsible for our reconciliation. Because of your suggestion, he came to me to talk about our differences."

Deborah looked up at him and smiled. "I'm so glad. He was such a troubled man. I'm sure he feels better after making his peace with you."

"He does. And so do I."

"Is that why you have come? Because Ophrah has released Beth-gader from his vow of blood revenge?"

Hareph hesitated. He looked steadily at Deborah, his face serious.

"No. Not really. I have come . . . to see you."

I knew exactly where this discussion was leading us, and I didn't like it. In fact, I resented it with all my being. I could feel the anger rising, in my blood, in my face.

A puzzled look came over Deborah's face. "You've come to see me? But — why?"

Hareph smiled. "Ophrah and I have decided to lay the matter before you and be guided by your wisdom."

"What?" My own voice surprised me. I stood up, laying my wine cup aside. "Hareph, you can't mean that. Why, you . . . you make it sound as though Deborah is Israel's shaphat! You know that isn't true. Shamgar is Israel's shaphat. You have no right to place this child in that position of responsibility."

"Be at peace, Beriah." Hareph raised his

hand, as though he were calming an angry dog. "Surely you know that Yahweh's wisdom is upon her. God may well have sent her to Israel for just these times. You've lived with her a full year. By now you surely know —"

"I know nothing of the sort, Hareph. My wife is nothing more than my wife. You have no right to make her into a . . . a —"

"A divinely appointed shaphat? No, I don't. Only God can do that. When will you recognize that?"

"But . . . but —"

I must have looked hostile to him. My fists opened and closed. There was undoubtedly a flush on my frowning face. My voice was sharp and whining.

Again he held up his hand. "All right, Beriah. If that's the way you feel about it, I won't insist that Deborah render judgment between us. But I would like to ask both of you for an opinion."

I must have realized in that moment how foolish I looked to him. He was a guest in my house. I had a reputation for being even-tempered and clear-headed. Now here I was losing my temper and indulging in a childish outburst. I was suddenly ashamed of myself.

"Well . . . ask us then. But Deborah is *not* a

shaphat of Israel. Let that be clearly understood."

"As you wish, Beriah. I shall only tell you about our dilemma. Nothing more."

I sat down. Nothing about this conversation seemed right to me, but what could I do?

Hareph continued. "As you know, Ophrah has sworn a sacred oath before Yahweh that he will execute the blood revenge against Beth-gader because of the death of his son. But we both realize now how unjust this is. Deborah, in her wisdom, has helped us see that."

He paused and looked at me uncertainly, wondering perhaps if this last comment would evoke another outburst of temper from me. I said nothing, but continued to glower at him.

He went on. "That blood vengeance. A sacred vow. Sworn before Yahweh. That's the problem."

Hareph pulled at his beard, frowning. After a short pause, he continued.

"Ophrah wanted to rescind it, but you know you can't do that."

Hareph was right. The blood revenge was a sacred oath which must be carried out. This tradition was even more ancient than the law of Moses. *An eye for an eye, a tooth for a tooth, a life for a life.*

Hareph sighed. "This is our dilemma. He wants out of the oath. Beth-gader's life is at stake. How do we do it?"

"There is only one way," I said sullenly. "The death of the high priest Maráioth the Levite, who lives in Shechem. He has assumed the responsibility for Beth-gader's guilt. When he dies, the 'life for a life' part of the oath will be satisfied. That is the law."

"Yes." Hareph continued to pull on his beard, which may have reflected his own anguish. "That's the problem. According to Ophrah, Maráioth the Levite is quite healthy, and probably will not die for many years."

Hareph glanced at me, then looked at Deborah. He opened his mouth to speak, but then turned and looked at me again. When he finally spoke, he addressed his words to me. "Tell me, Beriah, can you think of any way this can be resolved? Must we wait until Maráioth dies, or is there any other way?"

"There is no other way. Not even an animal sacrifice may be substituted. This is a blood vow. A life for a life. The law is very clear —"

"Please, sir. . . ." Deborah's soft voice contrasted with my own sharp one. She looked shyly at Hareph, then dropped her eyes.

"Yes, my dear?" Hareph reached out and

took her hand again. The gesture almost seemed to give her permission to speak.

Deborah hesitated. She stole a glance at me. I sighed, and said, "Go ahead, Deborah. Say what you want to say."

"Thank you, Beriah." She spoke so humbly and looked so demure I could hold no anger against her. In fact, I found myself eagerly waiting to hear what she would say.

"Would it be possible for Beth-gader to give his own life in place of the life he took? Wouldn't this fulfill the requirements of the law?"

Hareph frowned. "You mean commit suicide?"

"No sir. I mean, give his life while he still lives. Let Beth-gader take the place of the son Ophrah lost. If he could serve Ophrah as a servant — no, as a son — then maybe it would fulfill the requirement of the law which says that a life must be given for a life."

There followed a moment of breathless silence. Hareph stared at her. When he finally spoke, his voice reflected awe. "Ophrah did not exaggerate, my dear. God's wisdom is surely upon you."

Hareph's words touched something deep inside me which had been smoldering throughout this discussion. He had just implied once more that he wanted to make Deborah a shaphat in Israel. I would not have it. But what could I say?

I struggled for a rebuttal, and came up with a lame offering. "This can't be, Hareph. The law specifically states that the redemption of a life for a life must be made by the high priest, and him alone. It says nothing about someone else taking on the role of the redeemer."

Hareph turned to me, frowning. "That's true, Beriah. I hate to admit it, but what you say is right."

Again Deborah spoke, and now her voice was even softer. "That's true as to the *letter* of the law, but what about the *spirit* of the law? Isn't it more important to fulfill the spirit rather than the letter of the law? As long as a life is given for a life. . . ."

Hareph turned to her and spoke eagerly. "Yes, yes. You are right. Don't you agree, Beriah?"

He seemed so pathetically eager to accept this, I didn't have the heart to disillusion him. I smiled grimly. Let him believe what he wanted to believe. It made no difference to me.

"You may be right, my friend. As long as both you and Ophrah accept it," I said.

"I certainly accept it. And I know Ophrah

will also. In fact, we agreed before I came that —"

He broke off suddenly and turned aside. But not before I could see him biting his lip. I knew in a flash of insight what he was going to say. *We agreed to abide by Deborah's judgment.*

Again I felt cold rage creeping over my body. He was trying to steal my wife. Yes, steal my wife. He wanted to turn her around, from a wife and mother to a shaphat of Israel. I would not have it. But I would not allow myself to erupt again in a fit of temper.

Instead I spoke with cool deliberation. "Do as you please with your son. Return him to Ophrah if that is your wish. Let Bethgader serve Ophrah in place of his slain son. But —" Here I paused, to emphasize my next statement. "But do *not* — ever — come back expecting Deborah to make another judgment. And do not — ever — tell anyone else to come to Deborah for a judgment. Do you understand? She is my wife. She is *not* the shaphat of Israel!"

He looked steadily at me for a moment, no doubt evaluating the sincerity of my statement. At last he sighed. "It shall be as you say, Beriah." Then he turned to Deborah. "And you, my dear. Yahweh has indeed given you the gift of wisdom. Even if —" He glanced quickly at me. "Even if this is the only judgment you ever make."

Deborah clasped his hands in hers. "Go in peace, Father Hareph. May you and Ophrah both find peace. And may your son Beth-gader, who is now the son of both you and Ophrah, have a long and happy life serving you both. Yahweh has blessed you richly."

Hareph caught his breath, and I could see a tear forming in his eye. "Thank you, my dear. Thank you. Praise Yahweh!"

Suddenly I knew that, in spite of my harsh admonition to Hareph, this was not the end of the matter. I felt very insecure about the future. Would I perhaps lose my wife to . . . to serve as Israel's shaphat because of her wisdom? Her *God-given* wisdom?

12

Because I was able to concentrate fully on business affairs, my estate prospered. As the *malkosh* approached, when the rainy season would end, the crops which had been planted in several different fields ripened. The harvest was plentiful. Suddenly my livestock, already numerous, almost doubled as lambs, kids, calves, and colts seemed to spring from their mothers' wombs. I was already rich, but now I had become one of the most affluent landowners in all of Ephraim.

Yet I had no children.

For some men of Israel, this was enough to grant the wife a certificate of divorce, or to take another wife. I chose neither. My relationship with Deborah was so sweet I could not bear the thought of being without her, or even sharing her with another woman. So I placed my trust in the benevolent God who ruled Israel. I patiently waited for her to join the ewes, nannies, cows and she-asses with a fruitful womb.

During the dry season, I dug more wells.

The season was not a drought, but I was planning for the future. Sooner or later there would be a drought; when it came, I would have plenty of water. Besides, my growing number of servants needed something to do.

One of the tasks I assigned to my servants was to learn the martial arts. I hired Nubt-Re, a professional soldier from Egypt, to teach them how to handle a spear and sword. Thus not only did I have herdsmen, craftsmen, farmers, and household servants in my employ, but almost all of them became warriors.

This was a necessary step in these dangerous times. The widespread rumors seemed to be true. King Jabin of Hazor apparently *was* arming the Canaanites in the countryside and turning them against the Israelites.

I could almost understand the frustration of these Canaanites who took up arms for King Jabin. Most of them had been small farmers and herdsmen, but they had lost much of their land and herds due to poor management. They resented the Israelites, who had settled in their country. We were industrious, efficient, and wise in all our husbandry. The Canaanites were jealous of our prosperity.

Travel had become dangerous. Wherever we went we had to be accompanied by a contingent of at least twenty-one warriors. Every day as I traveled around my estate, I had a small army with me. Wherever I went I saw that the flocks and herds were guarded by more herdsmen than were needed, all armed and trained.

I came home one day tired but content. I had just enabled one of my herdsmen to retire. He and his wife had no sons, and the man was old and unable to work much. I had arranged for him to live in Bethel and provided food and lodging for as long as he and his wife lived. This was more than just charity on my part; it was good business. My employees would remain loyal to me and work hard because they knew I would take care of them.

As I entered the gates of my house, I noted with satisfaction the guards posted on the walls. The small army which followed me everywhere those days was dismissed to barracks. I went to the main house to find my wife.

Zimri stood at the door. The old servant had been watching for me. As soon as he saw me enter the gates, he hobbled out into the courtyard on legs bowed by arthritic knees. Old eyes peered out at me under white eyebrows.

"Sir," he said respectfully, "you have a visitor. No, you have two visitors. In fact, you have thirty visitors. But only two of them are important. The others are just their escort. They are now in the barracks, where they are now being fed and —"

"Zimri," I interrupted. If I hadn't, the garrulous servant would have explained every detail I didn't need to know. "Who are the two visitors in the house? What do they want?"

"I don't know what they want, sir. They wouldn't discuss their business until you arrived. I think they planned to talk to lady Deborah, but she insisted they wait until you came. I don't think they liked that very much, but she —"

"Zimri." Even though used to his eccentric ways, I found him exasperating at times. "Who are these men?"

"One is Jobab. I forget the other's name, but I think he's the son of Shimei. They're not Ephraimites, but I'm not sure where they're from. I am only a servant, so I didn't ask, and the lady Deborah insisted they wait —"

"Thank you, Zimri." I hurried past him and up the stairs to the upper room where we entertained guests.

The two men stood when I entered the room. They had been served wine, and I noticed that their feet were clean. My wife had performed the tasks of hospitality.

"Greetings, Beriah." The man who spoke first was tall and thin, his weather-beaten face lined with age. His hair was dusty from travel, and I noticed some gray at the temples. "I am Jobab ben Elpaal, from the tribe of Benjamin."

"And I," said the other, "am Eliel ben Shimei." He was squat and bald, about the same age as Jobab.

"Welcome, my friends. My house is your house, my servants will serve you. Please stay with us two nights and the day between."

"Thank you, Beriah." The taller man, Jobab, seemed the spokesman for the two. "You are very kind. Your wife is charming. We have a matter we would like to discuss with you."

"Let it wait until after dinner," I said. "Then we will all feel more like talking."

They accepted this, as was the custom. Deborah washed my feet. As she did, she gave me a troubled glance. Had these men said something to disturb her?

Mother and two servants served the meal, a goat roasted in herbs, with new cheese made of goat's milk and two kinds of bread. Deborah saw to it that our wine glasses were filled.

Talk during supper was mostly of the

growing threat of the Canaanites. They had seen several bands of armed men as they journeyed from Benjamin to Ephraim, but they were not attacked because of the strength of their guards. They were worried, as I was, about the future.

Finally the meal was finished and the dishes cleared away. We sat with our wine cups. The women and servants left the room.

"Please, Beriah," said Jobab. "Ask your wife to stay."

I frowned. Women had no place in a man's discussion. I didn't like the direction this would lead us. But I couldn't refuse the men this request.

"Deborah," I called. "Come here, please."

She appeared immediately, as though she had been waiting for my summons just outside the door. She sat on a bench near the door, gazing at the floor. Once she threw me a glance; I could see worry in her eyes.

Jobab took a deep breath. "Actually, Beriah, we have come to see Deborah. We seek her wisdom. But she would not speak to us unless you were present."

I looked at Deborah. "Thank you, my dear," I said to her. "That was wise."

Eliel cleared his throat. "But Beriah, it is Deborah whose wisdom we seek. She must judge a dispute between us."

I sat still. Maybe my face reflected the turmoil inside me. They studied me in silence.

So. It had come to this. Ophrah and Hareph had not kept silent about Deborah's wisdom, as they promised. And now these two men had come to steal my wife. In their minds she was no longer Beriah's wife; she was Israel's shaphat.

I sat in silence for another moment. I fought to control my feelings. I refused to lose my temper. No matter what developed in this conversation, I would remain calm. The men respected my silence, probably reading on my face the conflict within me.

Finally I spoke, and my words were slow and charged with emotion. "Please understand this, my friends. There has been a mistake. Deborah is *not* the shaphat of Israel. The rumors which have traveled from one tribe to another are false. Let there be no mistake about that. No woman, least of all my wife, shall sit in judgment in Israel."

"But Beriah, we have heard —"

"You have heard of Deborah's wisdom. Yes. But she is *not* Israel's shaphat. I forbid it."

"Beriah, be reasonable. We have come a long way —"

"It is not much farther to Beth-anath where Shamgar lives. *He* is Israel's shaphat."

Eliel snorted. "*He* is not Israel's shaphat.

He's just a brave man who killed some Canaanites with an ox goad. God never appointed him to sit in judgment —"

"How do you think God appoints shaphats?" I demanded. "He first gives them a military victory. This qualifies them to judge."

"You can't believe that, Beriah." Jobab's thin face was creased with a frown. "God gives people different talents. To some he gives military prowess. To others he gives wisdom. He never gave Shamgar wisdom. Everybody knows that."

"Nevertheless, he is Israel's shaphat. You must go —"

"No!" Eliel's voice was guttural. "We'll never get God's judgment from Shamgar. That's why we're here. God has given Deborah the gift of wisdom. We are in desperate need of it now."

"No!" My voice was as guttural as Eliel's. "I forbid it. No woman shall sit in judgment in Israel. Especially not my wife."

"You cannot deny that God has raised her up to lead Israel in these times, when there is no wise leader, when justice is neglected because of the lack of a judge. When God raised up a shaphat —"

"No wife of mine shall sit in judgment of Israel." I was repeating myself. This had gone beyond reason and logical discussion. I could only restate my position, forcefully, unequivocally.

A moment of silence followed my strong statement. Finally Jobab sighed. "Why don't we ask Deborah what she thinks?"

"All right," I said.

I knew what she would say. She had refused to talk to them this afternoon, choosing to wait until I came. She knew how I felt about this. I was confident of her answer.

She stared at the floor, but I could see tears running down her cheek. Suddenly I felt ashamed of myself and angry at these men. We were putting her through torment a young woman should not have to endure. We were arguing over her as though she were a lamb on sale.

Finally she looked up, and her round eyes stared at me. "Please, Beriah," she whispered. "You must not refuse what God has ordained."

I gasped. No. She could not be saying that. She could not believe God had appointed her to do this.

"Deborah," I said sternly. "You are *not* Israel's shaphat. You are my wife. Do you understand?"

She continued to stare at me. Tears dripped from her cheeks and fell on her breast, creating two wet spots. She made no move to wipe her eyes.

"I have before me," she said, speaking softly and slowly, "two distinct commands. My husband tells me to be his wife. But my God tells me to . . . to . . . be Israel's shaphat. I want to obey my husband. But I cannot. I must obey God."

I gaped at her. She could not be saying this. She was defying me, disobeying my explicit command. I started to say something, something harsh, a word of authority. But the words stuck in my mouth. My tongue would simply not function. I was struck dumb.

Silence hung like a heavy cloud in the room. No one moved. An eternity passed, although it was only a few seconds.

Finally Deborah rose from her bench and walked to me. Kneeling in front of me, she placed her hands on my lap. The look on her face drew from me not anger but pity. There was more anguish inside her than in me.

"Please, Beriah," she whispered, "I love you. I want to obey you. But I can't. I must obey God. And . . . I don't want you to try to change God's will."

As I looked into her face, wet with tears and torn by torment, I could not be angry with her. This was not her doing. She had been put in a position that was tearing her apart. She truly felt the choice was clear — obedience to her husband, or obedience to God. When it came to that kind of a choice, I could not possibly stand in her way.

"Deborah, my love," I whispered. I could feel tears starting in my own eyes.

"I know, Beriah. I know. You are afraid you are losing me. In a way you are. And I know what you must feel, because I feel much the same way myself. I don't want to lose you. But even so, I can't deny —"

"Yes. You can't deny God. But you can't deny my love, either. Do you think . . ." I wondered if I should say it so boldly. "Do you think you could love me and obey God at the same time? Be Israel's shaphat and my wife both? Is it possible?"

"We can try, Beriah. I *must* obey God, but I can't bear to lose you."

"Nor can I. So be it." I clasped her hands and sighed. "You are Israel's shaphat, then. But you are also my wife."

"Yes, Beriah. Thank you."

We had forgotten the other two men in the room. Wisely, they had remained silent while we settled our differences. Now Jobab spoke.

"Praise Yahweh! For he has raised up a shaphat."

"Yahweh's name be praised!" echoed Eliel.

143

I continued to stare at Deborah's face. Deep within her I could read her anguish. Being Israel's shaphat was not something she wanted to do. She did not seek the position. She had been divinely appointed, and she could not avoid it. And in doing so, her life's work had been assigned to her, whether she liked it or not.

"Tomorrow." My voice almost cracked. "Not tonight. She will begin her duties as Israel's shaphat tomorrow." I glanced at the two men. "Surely your business can wait until then."

They nodded.

"Zimri," I shouted. The old servant shuffled into the room. "We shall retire for the night. Show these men to their quarters."

Deborah remained on her knees before me while the two men followed Zimri out of the room. Then we stood and went to our bedroom.

Our lovemaking that night was a mixture of sadness and passion. We both knew a momentous change was about to take place. We didn't know what the future would bring, but we knew that this was the last night Deborah belonged to me wholly, as a full-time wife.

Tomorrow she would be the shaphat of Israel.

13

The next morning we met with Jobab and Eliel to hear their problem, which was a simple land dispute. Their common ancestor had divided his property equally among his descendants. Now Jobab and Eliel, cousins, disagreed on where the boundary line should be drawn.

It was an amiable disagreement. Neither of them showed any hostility toward the other. Deborah told me later she suspected they could easily have settled it between themselves, but they were curious to see the new shaphat of Israel.

Deborah's solution was to draw the boundary line directly through the center of the disputed territory. It was such an obvious resolution that the men accepted it immediately. Or did they accept it because Deborah presented it in such a charming way they could do nothing but accept it? In any case, they proclaimed Deborah to have God's true gift of wisdom.

When they left the next day, I did not ask

them to keep quiet about Deborah being the ordained shaphat of Israel. It would have done no good. With a feeling of helplessness, I accepted the fact that I had lost a wife to the public service of our people.

At first there was no change in our lives, but I knew change was coming. So did Deborah. She was saddened by that knowledge. We both knew we couldn't go against what we believed was the will of God for Israel.

Two weeks after the visit by Jobab and Eliel, two more men appeared at our gates, petitioning Deborah for a judgment. Azel ben Jeush and Hanan ben Hushim were not quite as amiable as Jobab and Eliel had been. In fact, they were belligerent.

"We agreed to abide by Deborah's decision," said Azel, darting frowning glances at his companion.

"But that's all we agreed on," retorted Hanan brusquely.

I wondered what effect their hostility toward each other would have on Deborah. Her previous petitioners had been pleasant and agreeable, but these men were antagonistic. Would their animosity carry over in their attitude toward their shaphat?

It did. I sensed it as they presented their problem.

Azel paced the courtyard and spoke

gruffly. "My son wants to marry Hannah *bath* Moshes. Moshes agreed to this before Hanan came along."

"That makes no difference, Deborah." Hanan stood unmoving, his voice curt and scornful. "Moshes agreed to my offer. There was nothing binding in the previous betrothal agreement because the *mohar* had never been paid. Moshes had a right to re-negotiate if he wants to."

That was by no means clear in the law. The *mohar*, the bride-price paid by the fa-ther of the bridegroom, could be seen as binding whether the money actually ex-changed hands or not. On the other hand, since it was not paid, the bride's father might be free to renegotiate. It was more a matter of honor than legality.

How would Deborah handle this? I knew instantly what I would do. I would rule in favor of Azel, the one who first made the be-trothal contract with Moshes. Legally, it could go either way. But when honor was involved, I would hold Moshes to his original promise.

Deborah had other ideas. "Return home," she told them. "I will not judge this on the basis of what you have told me. Instead, I ask that you send me Moshes and his daughter. I will give him my judgment, and he will then tell you which one Hannah will marry."

Azel and Hanan grumbled at this decision, but, surprisingly, they accepted it. They left, promising to send Moshes and his daughter Hannah to Deborah for judgment.

After they left, I confronted Deborah. "The issue was clear," I stated firmly. "You should have ruled for Azel, who had the prior claim. A matter of honor —"

"Please, Beriah." The humility in her voice drew my attention. She was not trying to be disrespectful to me, but I knew she did not agree. "Honor is not involved."

"Then what is?" I demanded.

"Happiness," she replied.

"Happiness? Whose? And what does that have to do with it?"

She shook her head. "I don't know yet. Not until I have talked with Moshes and Hannah. Let's wait and see."

We waited. A week later, they came. Moshes was a wealthy man, in poor health, carried by servants on a chair. Hannah was a child, beautiful, bashful — but charming. We entertained them and their guards for two nights and the day in between.

Deborah confronted them in the morning. Rain fell, and we gathered in the upper room. It was a dreary morning.

"Which one, Father Moshes, do you want your daughter to marry?" she asked.

"The son of Hanan," he replied instantly. "Why?"

He shrugged. "Better family. More property, larger flocks, more servants. His *mohar* is higher. Hannah will be much happier in his household."

I recalled Deborah's statement that the issue was happiness. Was this what she meant?

Deborah would not give a judgment at first. She questioned Moshes at length, learning about him and his household. He obviously cared a great deal about his daughter . . . and her happiness.

Deborah promised to give a judgment the next morning before they left.

Before supper, Deborah and Hannah went off together, leaving Moshes and me to discuss the growing threat of the Canaanites. Moshes had heard rumors of King Jabin of Hazor and his chariots.

"Chariots?" I asked, surprised.

"Chariots. I understand he has developed quite a chariot corps."

We discussed this until it was time for supper. We discussed it during supper, and after supper. We did not discuss the problem they had come here with, though I was sure Deborah and Hannah discussed it.

The next morning Deborah and I met

with them in the courtyard as they were pre-paring to leave. Their twenty-one armed guards stood waiting just outside the gates while we said good-bye.

Then Deborah gave them her judgment. "Hannah shall marry the son of Azel," she said firmly. "I believe this is the will of Yahweh. Only in this marriage will they find happiness."

Moshes opened his mouth, closed it, swallowed, and opened it again. "Why?" he muttered.

Deborah would not answer. Instead she went to Hannah and grasped both her hands. "I wish you the best of everything, my dear. Please come to visit me some time."

Hannah smiled, and it was the first time since their arrival that I had seen her do so. Her face lit up, her eyes shone, and her chin lifted regally. "Thank you, Mother Deborah. You are so good and kind."

As I gave the ritual words of farewell to Moshes, I was perplexed. The judgment pleased Hannah and disturbed Moshes.

When they had gone, I turned to Deborah, smiling. "It *was* a matter of honor, after all. The man with the prior agreement took pre-cedence."

"No, Beriah." She came to me, shyly, and reached for my hand. "It was a matter of happiness. Hannah's happiness. She told me about the two young men who want to make her their wife. It wasn't hard to know which one she would be happier with."

"But — how can you tell that? Wouldn't happiness come with the security of a wealthier household?"

She looked into my eyes, and said slowly, "Beriah . . . my love. You have taught me so much in the past two years about love . . . and happiness. I want that for Hannah. That and only that."

I recalled the words Hannah had said just before she left. She had called Deborah "Mother," a term of respect for an older woman, although Deborah was only sixteen.

When I looked into her eyes, I understood what she had just told me. I caught my breath. This was not Deborah, the wise shaphat of Israel. This was Deborah, my wife, my beloved. She had used our marriage, our love, as her guide to Hannah's happiness.

I took her in my arms. "Deborah, my love."

She responded by turning her face up to be kissed. The kiss I placed on her lips was tender.

"You may be the shaphat of Israel," I said. "But you're still my wife."

"Yes, Beriah. Yes. Always."

But I think we both knew it could not be.

14

At first there was little change in our lives. While petitioners came for Deborah's wisdom, I continued to go about my business managing the estate. Deborah and I still maintained the normal life of husband and wife and hoped this would never change.

During the first year Deborah was the shaphat, I tried to be present as people came to her. I thought it was my duty as host. It seemed improper that a woman should stand alone in the place of judgment. Although the wisdom came from her, I was always there, acting as host, as coordinator, as the man of the household to smooth the proceedings. As time went by, however, and more and more petitioners came, the business of my estate began to suffer. I could not neglect it.

A new pattern began to emerge. Each day Deborah and I left home together to go about our separate affairs. I went with a group of twenty-one guards to the various parts of my estate, to supervise the breeding of the flocks, to oversee the planting, to settle disputes, to buy and sell. Deborah, weather permitting, went to our palm tree which she had made her judgment seat. There she judged Israel.

I saw to it that she was well guarded. Thirty-five of my warriors stationed themselves up and down the road between my house and Ramah, near the small grove of my palm tree. Even though she was outside the walls of my house, she felt relatively secure from any Canaanite threat. Not only was she guarded by my warriors, but she was constantly surrounded by the people of Israel who came to her, along with their guards.

Old Zimri, the useless household servant, suddenly became useful. He took my place as the male host in the place of judgment. He greeted all newcomers, welcomed them, provided them with refreshments, and ushered them into Deborah's presence when their turn came. As soon as one petitioner finished, he brought in the next, then said farewell to the one leaving. Because of him, I felt I could leave and go about my business.

Deborah told me about her petitioners. She did so with excitement. At first she was hesitant, lacking self-confidence. But as time went on, and her wisdom led to satisfactory solutions to the problems presented to her, her confidence grew and she talked with more assurance about her work.

The people came from all over Israel. From the tribe of Zebulon came a man who claimed a large tract of land. His uncle, who previously owned it, died with no sons to inherit. He was the only living heir. But other greedy relatives wanted a part of it, and he wanted Deborah to tell them that he and he only had a rightful claim to the property.

Under questioning, the Zebulonite admitted that his uncle, who had no sons, did have two daughters. Deborah promptly awarded the property to the two girls and their husbands, citing a precedent from the time of Moses. The original Zebulonite went away very unhappy, but he was a true Israelite and accepted the ruling of Israel's shaphat.

From the tribe of Asher, a slave petitioned Deborah for freedom for himself and his family. According to the law of Moses, he had the right to be set free after serving seven years. Under questioning, Deborah learned that his master had given him his wife. Technically, she belonged to the master, but Deborah was unwilling to separate a married couple, especially since they had children.

When Deborah noticed that the man had a pierced ear, she immediately ruled that the slave could not leave his master. That was the law: when a slave voluntarily chose to serve his master beyond the mandatory seven years, his ear was pierced. This man had obviously made that choice some time in the past and therefore was bound to his master for life. However, she directed the master to give the slave more responsibility and respect, since he was no ordinary slave.

From the tribe of Simeon came a man whose crops had failed. He had borrowed from a neighbor to see him and his family through the year. The crops had failed again, and the neighbor demanded repayment by claiming the debtor and his family as slaves. Deborah ruled that the man and his family must serve their neighbor for seven years, but reminded them of the law which said that the land must lie fallow one year out of seven, which was the reason the crops failed. The land, like the people who till it, must rest. This was not only the law of Moses, but the law of God.

From Reuben came a man who claimed that his new wife was not a virgin. In fact she was three months pregnant when he married her, but he did not realize that until the child was born early. The actual father of the child was a neighbor, who had seduced the girl before her marriage, while she was betrothed to the Reubenite. The man insisted that his wife and baby be executed by stoning for her adultery, but Deborah refused to grant the request. She ruled instead that the man give his wife a certificate of divorce, and that she marry the true father of the child.

And so they came, from Naphtali and Manassah and Gad, from Judah and Benjamin and Dan, seeking wisdom and impartiality. Most of them brought simple cases of Mosaic Law. But in some cases one was telling the truth and the other wasn't. Deborah ruled firmly in these cases, although at times she sent a petitioner back to bring forth more witnesses.

That these people accepted her judgments was remarkable. I marveled at her wisdom. A large part of her appeal was her charm and humility. Even those who lost a case seemed to love her and accepted her judgment merely on the basis of Deborah's personality.

I was also struck by the fact that most of the petitioners came seeking only a voice of authority. Their disputes were petty, the solutions obvious, but they needed Israel's shaphat to rule on them before they would accept.

What surprised me most was that the people who came to Deborah for judgment did not resent the fact that the shaphat of Israel was a woman. They merely accepted the fact that God had given her wisdom and had divinely appointed her to the job. Who were they to question the mysterious decree of Yahweh?

As the years passed, more and more people came to Deborah. Sometimes she could not see all of them in one day. She came to me at night exhausted. More often than not, she was too tired to indulge in the beautiful ecstasy which makes a joy of the married couple's bed. I became increasingly aware that my wife had been stolen from me by the people of Israel.

At first we tried to preserve the Sabbath as our day to be together. She refused to sit in judgment on the seventh day, proclaimed by Moses as the Sabbath, the day of rest. Then a new custom developed. Petitioners would come on the day before the Sabbath, and when she could not see them before sundown, she would make them wait until the day after the Sabbath. As a result we entertained them on our day of rest.

To fill in the time, Deborah would sing for them. The poems I had written which she had put to music had been sung for me

157

alone. But now she shared them with Israel. She would meet with our guests at our palm tree and there talk and sing and generally entertain them. Always I sat on the edge of the crowd, patiently waiting, often brooding.

The small grove containing the palm tree had changed. It was no longer the place of serenity and beauty. Trampled by many feet, it now resembled the courtyard of a house. The gentle spring now became a muddy pathway. The lark was gone.

The people called the place, "Deborah's palm tree." It seemed symbolic of the changes which had taken place in our household. At first this was my palm tree, where I went to find peace and compose my empty poems. Then it became our palm tree, where Deborah and I together shared many beautiful moments.

Now it was Deborah's palm tree. She was not my wife anymore. She was married to Israel.

15

"Modan," I said to my nephew, "I want you to be my steward."

Modan stood before me in the courtyard at my house in Ramah. I had just arrived; it was early in the morning.

He raised his eyebrows. "But Beriah, what about Tola?"

Tola had been the steward of the estate since the time of my father. He had always been efficient and hardworking but never imaginative or resourceful. He had needed someone to tell him what to do. My father had done it until his death, and since then I was his supervisor.

"Tola has grown old and cannot handle the physical exertion required in this job. The last time we went to the valley beyond Bethel, he was so exhausted when we returned that he could not work the next day."

Modan nodded. "What will Tola do?"

I liked the way Modan showed concern for the person he would be replacing. He had always been a thoughtful youth, concerned about the welfare of others. I looked at him fondly. When his father died ten years ago, he was a beardless youth, full of energy and enthusiasm. Now, in maturity, he was heavily bearded, tall, and gifted with a commanding presence.

"Tola will manage my household in Bethel," I said. "I want you to manage my estate."

"Do you think I can handle it?"

I smiled. "We'll see." But I knew he could. Unlike his father Rakem, he showed no warlike tendencies. He was good at keeping accounts and managing people.

We went together that day to one of my fields near Ramah. A well had failed, and there had been no rain for several weeks, even though it was the rainy season. We began the task of digging a new well and diverting a stream into the field. The shepherds were working on it when we left.

It was only a few miles to Ramah. We walked along the road in the afternoon sunshine, expecting to be home before sundown, the beginning of the Sabbath. I scanned the skies, hoping to see a cloud which promised rain.

We topped a rise and looked out across the valley. The road branched off there, the northern road going toward Ramah and

Bethel, the western branch toward Gaza and the Canaanite cities on the Great Sea.

Modan grasped my arm. "Beriah! Look!"

He pointed ahead. In the distance, coming from the west, was a chariot.

I stopped, gaping. I had seen a few of them before, but I never paid much attention. Israelites did not own them. They were Canaanite vehicles.

"Nubt-Re," I shouted. "What shall we do?"

The Egyptian soldier trotted forward and stood beside us, calmly watching the oncoming chariot. He shaded his eyes.

"Sir," he said, his accent thick, "we kill horse first. Then men. Must do quick; they come fast."

"No," I said. "Maybe they will talk. How do we signal them that we are peaceful?"

Nubt-Re snorted. "They not peaceful. Best way stop them, spear-point. You watch. I show."

He knelt on the road and thrust the butt end of his spear into the dirt. He lowered the point until it was about the height of the horses' breast.

"Need four more. You. You." He pointed to five of our men. They came forward and aligned their spears as he had done.

I nodded. That would stop them. Once stopped, we would talk. But Nubt-Re had more on his mind than talk.

"You men. Go down road. Both sides. Take cover. Be ready to charge with spear."

"Don't fight until they fire their arrows," I ordered.

Nubt-Re frowned. His theory was to attack first. But he was under my orders, and he was a good soldier.

"If they shoot first," he said, "we kill horses."

I agreed. This was good strategy. The advantage of a chariot was its maneuverability. Without the horses, the enemy was no more than three men — against our twenty-one.

The chariot approached, the two horses trotting. We could see the three men in it — the driver, the warrior, and the shield bearer. The driver was of course weaponless, but the other two had bows. I watched aghast as they fitted arrows to the bows.

Nubt-Re lifted his voice. "If they shoot arrows, attack. First kill horses, then fight men up close."

The men would see the reason for that. The archer had the advantage when there was a distance separating the combatants. But in hand-to-hand fighting, bows and arrows were useless.

Our men were deployed now, on either side of the road, crouching down behind rocks, trees, or any cover they could find. Five stalwart men stood in the center of the road, their spears set for the attack of the chariot.

But the men in the chariot knew better than to charge the set spears. Instead they came to a full stop and began to fire their arrows.

The first arrow caught one of my men in the throat. He gave a gagged cry, jerked spasmodically, and fell to the ground, clutching the arrow. Blood spurted from his throat. Our men wore no armor. They watched, openmouthed, as the two aimed their next arrows.

"Charge, you fools!" shouted Nubt-Re.

He leaped forward with his spear, recklessly running toward the enemy. He didn't have to run far, only about twenty paces. Then he plunged his spear into the chest of one of the horses.

His daring exploit galvanized the men into action. They leaped forward, shouting, their spears held firmly. The other horse was killed, and the charioteers leaped from their now useless chariot. They discarded their bows in favor of spears.

Twenty-one against three. It wouldn't have been much of a contest, except that one Canaanite warrior was a superb spear fighter. But he met his match in the professional soldier from Egypt. They did the spear dance for a while — thrusting, parrying, maneuvering — until one of my men hurled his spear at the Canaanite. It entered his body between his breastplate and helmet. He fell dead on the ground. My men had already killed his two companions.

I began to shake, gasping for breath. I had done nothing, yet I felt as though I had fully participated in the fierce battle. Modan, I saw, was shaken also.

Nubt-Re came toward us, grinning. "I teach men to use these!" he said, holding up the bow and arrows he had taken from the chariot. "Next time, we shoot horses. Make fight easier."

I breathed a silent prayer to Yahweh that this experienced warrior was with us. Without him, we would have been killed. Slaughtered by the deadly chariot.

Nubt-Re was right. We must somehow prepare for a war against chariots. If the bow and arrow was the answer, then we must adopt that weapon.

Modan knelt beside the body of our dead guard. "Hezron ben Nathan," he muttered. He shook his head. "His wife has no sons."

It was like Modan to be concerned. He would make an excellent steward.

"We'll find another husband for her," I said. "Does Hezron have any brothers?"

Modan nodded. "One. Shobal of Ramah, the potter. Do you think he will take her? He already has a wife and three sons."

"He'll take her. I'll see to that."

It would be hard for a potter to support so large a family. I decided I would order from him a whole new set of servingware for my house. Let Mother select the pattern; she would like that. And I would give him as much business as possible in the future.

Yes, Shobal would marry his brother's widow. It was the law. Moses said if a man dies childless, the brother of the deceased must marry the widow. I would see to it that Shobal obeyed the law.

Or better yet, I would have Deborah tell him. He would obey the shaphat of Israel.

16

Sundown, the beginning of the Sabbath, was cloudy with a promise of rain. We were well into the rainy season, but the land was dry. I was concerned about the crops.

The Sabbath, however, was not the time to worry about business matters. Like all true Israelites, we observed the Sabbath strictly. At sundown all work ceased. Food had been prepared for the next day, and only the most necessary chores, such as milking the cows and goats, were done. This included not only the servants, but also the stranger within our gates. And these days, there were plenty of them.

As the shadows crept over the courtyard, we served our guests the pre-prepared meal. Then as was our custom, Deborah and I went to bed.

Although many Israelites had established the custom of abstaining from sexual relations during the time from sundown to sundown which marked the Sabbath, we had never followed the practice. It was not forbidden by the law, but some Israelites felt that abstinence obeyed the spirit of the law.

There were two reasons for the law of the Sabbath. One was rest; the human body needs one day out of seven to recover from the strenuous work of the other six days. The other reason was to honor God, and to remember his great works in bringing his people out of the land of Egypt and establishing us in our Promised Land.

Anything we could do to rest and honor Yahweh fulfilled the spirit of the Sabbath law, but neither of us felt abstinence from sexual relations in any way violated the spirit of the law. Sex was not work; it was pleasure, and the law certainly did not forbid pleasure. And the creative act of making a child did not seem to us a way to dishonor our Creator.

Too often on Sabbath evenings, however, Deborah had been too tired. Today, for example, she had met with fourteen petitioners, dispensing justice, pouring out her wisdom and strength. Six consecutive days of judging Israel had taken their toll. Tonight she was interested in neither sex nor sleep. In spite of her weariness, she wanted to hear more about my adventures today.

I told her in detail our experiences on the road with the chariot. I ended with the question which had caused me a moment of guilt. "Should we have attacked first? It might have saved poor Hezron's life."

She pursed her lips, thinking about this. "No," she replied, speaking slowly. "You did the right thing, Beriah. If you could have looked into the future and known that by attacking first, Hezron would still be alive, you would have done it. But you couldn't. You had to act on principle; that is always best, even though sometimes it causes us pain and guilt later."

"I'm not too sure. Maybe Nubt-Re is right about attacking first. Sometimes the aggressor has a distinct advantage."

"And what will you do next time?" she asked.

"Nubt-Re will teach our warriors to use the bow and arrow." I smiled grimly. "We'll probably attack first and kill the horses."

She shuddered. "Beriah, this can't go on. Chariots on the road, attacking innocent travelers, turning peaceful citizens into bloodthirsty killers of men and horses."

I put my arms around her. "It mustn't concern you, my dear. You have enough on your mind, judging Israel. You can't —"

I was about to say, "You can't be a mother to all Israel." But I checked myself. That was exactly what she was trying to do. She

168

couldn't mother my children. So she had adopted all Israel as her own.

Almost as though she read my thoughts, she laid her head on my shoulder and whispered, "I'm sorry, Beriah."

I held her tightly. I couldn't blame her for the situation. In that moment I came closer to cursing God than I ever had in my life. These were God's plans, God's arrangements. Deborah and I were his toys, which he moved around at will in the game of life. We had no control over the game. All we could do was play our little parts in it.

The next day we woke to rain. Finally the dry spell had ended and the rain we so much needed soaked the land. I wondered how this would change the situation in the pasture south of Ramah, where we had dug that well the day before. I felt guilty even thinking these thoughts today. Not just my body but also my mind should rest on the Sabbath.

The upper room where we entertained our guests was warm and cozy, in spite of the dampness and chill outside. Old Zimri had kindled a small blaze in the brazier, and Mother made sure bread, cheese, and beer were on the table. Even so, our guests were quiet and moody when Deborah and I joined them, possibly reflecting the dreariness of the weather.

Deborah's presence was like sun breaking through clouds. Her quiet cheerfulness, her broad smile, her obvious interest in each person as an individual, was endearing to everyone.

"Father Jehu," she said, advancing to a tall, middle-aged man with a bushy black beard. "I hope you slept well last night?"

Jehu ben Joshibiah, from Hebron in Judah, had come yesterday to talk to Deborah about his daughter's marriage. Because the Sabbath had begun when we met him last night, we could not learn details of his problems. Deborah would not allow him to discuss it until the Sabbath ended.

There were four other men in the room. Three of them had come together, from the tribe of Manassah, with a property dispute to be settled by Israel's shaphat. The other man, a Zebulonite, was taciturn and morose, refusing to talk to anyone about his problem.

Deborah was the only woman in the room, other than my mother, who came in and out with refreshments. Jehu, the Judahite, was the only one inclined to talk, and he wanted to talk to Deborah. I wondered if he would try to bring up his problem on the Sabbath, even though he knew that was forbidden.

But Jehu had no intention of discussing his

daughter's marriage. He wanted to talk about the Canaanites. "I was attacked on the road yesterday," he said loudly. Instantly he had the attention of everyone in the room.

"How many?" I asked.

"About twenty. We ran."

I knew he had brought with him a guard of twelve warriors. Right now they were being entertained in the barracks with my own men. I assumed Nubt-Re would be squeezing information from them which might be of help in planning military strategy. My job would be to squeeze political information out of Jehu.

"That was prudent. There is no need to fight, especially against overwhelming odds. How were they armed?"

Jehu's bushy beard seemed to bounce off his chest. "Spears, swords, and shields. They wore breastplates and helmets."

"The helmets," I asked. "Were they metal or leather?"

"Metal."

I nodded. "King Jabin's men."

"No."

We all grew quiet. Everyone knew King Jabin was arming the Canaanites to harass the Israelites. My question and his response about metal helmets were normal in every discussion about this universal problem of our times. But Jehu obviously knew something more, something the rest of us didn't know.

Jehu seemed to enjoy being the center of attention. He kept us waiting a few seconds before he answered.

"I understand there's another king we need to worry about now."

"Who?"

Jehu thrust out his beard. "Sisera."

"Sisera?" I frowned. The name was foreign. "Who's he?"

Jehu shrugged. "Some new king I heard about. He's from the north, near the Great Sea. I don't know much about him, except that it's he, not King Jabin, who's arming the Canaanites against us."

"Strange, that we've never heard about him." I looked around at the other men. "Have any of you heard of him?"

"I have."

The man who spoke was the quiet Zebulonite. He was young, handsome, his short black beard and dark eyes set in a mass of curly black hair. He had told us his name last night, but I had forgotten.

Deborah had not. "Amittai ben Shelesh," she said softly. "Tell us what you know about Sisera."

Amittai hesitated. He glanced at me, his host. I wondered if he were shy. Or was he so angry about the problem he had brought to the shaphat of Israel that he was preoccupied and morose?

"Please, my friend," I said. "Tell us. You will help us greatly if you do."

Amittai turned to Deborah. "I don't know if I should speak of this on the Sabbath."

Deborah nodded. She reached out and touched the young man's hand. "Is it because this concerns the problem you have brought here for my judgment?"

"Yes."

In that case, his news should properly be left until tomorrow. But I couldn't wait. Neither, I knew, could Jehu and the others.

"Tell us what you know, my friend," I said. "We need to know about this new threat to our safety."

He looked at me, and also at the others in the room. I had given him my permission as host to discuss a subject forbidden on the Sabbath. Perhaps he had personal problems which should properly be put off until tomorrow, but he could at least speak in general terms about the danger which surrounded us all.

He nodded, seemingly making up his mind.

"All right," he said. His voice was a deep bass, and very self-assured. "Sisera is one of the Sea People. He moved inland last year, and now his base of operations is in Harosheth."

"Harosheth?" Jehu raised an eyebrow. "Isn't that on the Plain of Ezdraelon? I knew someone from there. I met him three years ago."

"He doesn't live there now," said Amittai. "Or else he's dead. We call it Harosheth-Hagoiim now." Hagoiim. City of foreigners. The name had an ominous sound.

"Sisera," said Amittai, speaking slowly in a resonant voice, "is preparing for an all-out war against Israel."

A sudden cold silence gripped the room. We all stared at the man from Zebulon.

Finally Jehu spoke, in a hushed tone. "How long has this been going on?"

"Last year he attacked Harosheth. He either drove us out or killed us. He killed my father. Just last month he attacked Gath-Hepher, where we had fled for refuge. He burned our homes. My mother died in the fire. My sister was raped and beaten to death. I found them when I returned from the fields."

"Oh!" Deborah went to him and took both his hands in hers. "I'm so sorry."

The harsh features on Amittai's darkly handsome face softened. In place of the old man look, he became a child. For a moment

I thought he would cry.

I was holding my breath. Amittai's revelation had shocked me profoundly, as it had the others. Jehu stared at the young man, and the other three men came forward, frowning.

Amittai, however, wasn't finished. "Sisera and Jabin have formed an alliance," he continued. "They plan to drive out Israel from our Promised Land."

"How do you know that?" I demanded.

"One of the men from Gath-Hepher — one of the few who survived — recognized one of the commanders. He was an officer in King Jabin's army. And besides, Jabin is supplying Sisera with chariots."

"Chariots!" The word exploded from my lips.

Amittai nodded. "He's collecting them at Harosheth. Reports vary as to how many. Some say as many as nine hundred, but that's exaggerated."

"Have you seen any chariots?" I asked.

"On the way here yesterday, I was attacked by one. I was alone, so I escaped by climbing into the hills."

I recalled then that Amittai had arrived at my gates after sundown last night, without escort, and on foot.

"Describe the chariot," I said.

Amittai spoke confidently. "Two horses, three men. The chariot had a wickerwork body. The men were armed with both spears and bow and arrows. They wore metal helmets."

I nodded. "Hazorian. I was attacked yesterday by one myself."

"What happened?" demanded Jehu.

"Fortunately, I wasn't alone. My mercenary, Nubt-Re, knew what to do. My men deployed and were able to kill the Hazorians."

Jehu began to pace nervously. "Something must be done — and soon. These attacks have been going on for years, but now, with chariots, King Jabin and this Sisera have an advantage. Israel is in great danger."

"You're right," I replied. "When they were only small parties of Canaanites harassing us, it was no more than an inconvenience. Now, with chariots, the situation has become desperate."

Amittai spoke now, his youthful features earnest. "That's why I'm here. We need help. I have come to the shaphat of Israel to appeal for that help."

Everyone turned to Deborah, who stood quietly on the fringe of this conversation. Although she was Israel's shaphat, she was a woman, and this was men's talk. Settling petty disputes was one thing, but this involved war. And war was men's business.

I had to stop this. Bad enough to lose my wife to Israel because Yahweh had called her to be the shaphat. But no more. She would not become Israel's champion in battle.

Then I thought of a way to stop this. At least temporarily, until I thought of a way to discuss war without involving Deborah.

"In my house," I said slowly and with emphasis, "we do not speak of such matters on the Sabbath. Tomorrow morning let us meet at Deborah's palm tree and discuss what we shall do. But today let us keep the Sabbath. Deborah, sing us one of the songs of Israel."

I noticed hesitation in the faces of the men in the room. I understood how they felt. They were Israelites who respected the Sabbath laws. Yet the law allowed for some leeway when the situation was an emergency urgent enough to justify exceptions. Their dilemma was whether we should observe the Sabbath piously or discuss the urgent problem of the Canaanite threat.

But I was the host. This was my house. They had no choice but to observe the Sabbath. The problems of war could wait until tomorrow.

Deborah obviously thought so too. She had brought her lyre to the upper room, expecting to play and sing for her guests. This was the day to recall the heritage of Israel, to praise the God who brought us out of the land of Egypt, out of slavery, and into prosperity in our Promised Land. It was a day to be happy, to sing, to rejoice and offer the thanksgiving of our hearts to Yahweh.

As soon as Deborah plucked the strings of her instrument and the golden notes filled the room, all of us began to relax. I could sense the tension evaporating as we seated ourselves on the benches and turned to Deborah. She began to sing in that sweet, quiet voice which I loved so much, and which I now shared with Israel. "I will sing to the Lord, for he has triumphed gloriously; the horse and its rider he has thrown into the sea."

All of us instantly recognized the psalm she had chosen to sing. It was Miriam's song, describing the escape of the people of Israel when Moses parted the waters of the sea. This was one of the oldest and most beloved of all our psalms. What a wonderful way to enjoy the Sabbath, as we reflected on the great God who brought us to where we were today.

Instead of relaxing us, however, the song seemed to do just the opposite. There was a sense of excitement in the melody, especially the way she sang it now. Pharaoh's chariots charged into the waters which had been rolled back to form a wall on either side. There they were destroyed.

The sweet voice rose in intensity, urgently, describing the great victory over our enemies in that long ago but not forgotten day. I felt the stabbing excitement course through my body, and I sensed the others felt the same.

Who is like you, Yahweh, among the gods?
Who is like you, majestic in holiness,
    terrible in glorious deeds, doing wonders?
All the people of Canaan melt with fear;
Terror and dread fall upon them,
Yahweh, because of your great power
    they will not attack us.
You will plant them on your mountain,
    the sanctuary you made for them to live in.
Yahweh shall reign for ever and ever!

I knew then what she was doing. So did all the others in the room. She was celebrating the Sabbath, recalling our national history, offering praise to Yahweh. But she was doing much more. She was mobilizing Israel for war.

Even as I thrilled to the stirring message of her song, and swelled with pride in the greatness of Israel and Israel's God, I could not help but frown. She was Israel's judicial shaphat. But was she also Israel's military leader?

Would my wife go off to war? Would she be called upon to do what all other shaphats have done — captain the army that fights our enemies?

No. Never. I vowed I would do all I could to see that this would not happen.

17

Rain fell during the night. We could not meet at Deborah's palm tree the next morning.

I sent out runners to all my neighbors inviting them to come to the meeting. They came. Besides the usual petitioners who had come to Deborah for judgment, about twenty of my neighbors came. That was an indication of how seriously the problem of the Canaanite threat was taken.

The upper room where we entertained guests would not hold them all, nor would the commons room of the main house. Some gathered around the courtyard, seeking shelter under the eaves of the balcony. Mother and I served them bread and cheese and drinks.

Deborah met with the petitioners in our bedchamber, the only place we could think of where she would have some privacy. I was present for only one case, two people from Gad who had a simple property dispute. They were emotionally distraught, angry, and loud in their accusations against each other. Most of Deborah's petitioners were calm, polite, and quiet. When two irate men came to Deborah's judgment seat, I made sure either I or some other responsible man of my household was present.

This time the two men hurled accusations at each other, calling names, raising their voices. Not even Deborah's quiet humility could calm them. At one point I spoke sharply to them, reminding them that as long as they were guests in my house, they would speak respectfully in the presence of my wife. They grumbled but obeyed, not only because she was my wife and they were our guests, but also out of respect for the shaphat of Israel.

I knew from past experience that this kind of emotional situation was difficult for Deborah. Absorbing hostility drained her strength. Yet that did not prevent her from rendering a reasonable judgment, dividing the property equitably, and lecturing conflicting parties to be good neighbors according to the traditions of Israel.

By noon, the rain stopped, although clouds swirled in the sky with the promise of more. By then about forty men of Israel had come to our house, waiting for Deborah to speak to them about our common problem.

I directed our servants to place two chairs

in the center of the muddy courtyard. Deborah and I took our places there, while the people crowded around us. This was a strange tradition, that the shaphat should sit while the others stood. Deborah once guessed it was because as the shaphat grew old, he needed to rest. I could readily believe that, because judging Israel was a tiring job.

As the host, I opened the discussion. "Men of Israel." I spoke loudly, although they were respectfully quiet and could hear plainly enough. "Many of you have been attacked by Canaanites. Now they are using chariots."

I looked around at the frowning faces of these Israelites gathered here. All of them knew of the Canaanite threat. Few knew about the chariots, and fewer still about Sisera.

"Two days ago I was attacked on the road south of Ramah by a Hazorian chariot. We killed the Hazorians. Amittai ben Shelesh of Zebulon has reported many chariots collected in the city of Harosheth in Jezreel."

"You must do something, Beriah!" The man who spoke was my neighbor, Ashvath. He was a cantankerous old man who shunned responsibility. "These Canaanites must be stopped. King Jabin must be taught to respect Israel."

"We must all do something, Ashvath. But it is not just King Jabin. There's someone else. Sisera."

They waited. After a pause I resumed my speech, telling them what Amittai had told us yesterday about this new threat to Israel. When I finished, they stood silently for a moment, then erupted in a confused babbling.

"Sisera! A foreigner!"

"A worshiper of false gods!"

"He mocks Yahweh and Israel!"

"We're all in danger!"

"What shall we do?"

"Yes, what shall we do?"

Jehu ben Joshibiah, the Simeonite, raised the question which brought silence to the crowd of men in the courtyard.

"We want Israel's shaphat to tell us what to do. Deborah. You have God's wisdom. What must be done to save Israel?"

The babbling ceased immediately, as all eyes turned to Deborah. Until that moment she had said nothing. The talk of war was men's talk. In a crowd of men like this, she was naturally shy.

Before she spoke, she turned and beckoned to Old Zimri. She whispered something to him, which only I was close enough to hear: "Bring me my lyre."

As Old Zimri hobbled off on his errand, she took a deep breath, almost as though trying to gather courage to speak. When she finally spoke, her voice was soft, yet easily heard in the silence.

"We must organize for war."

Again, the babble of voices broke out.

"Against chariots?"

"Who will lead us?"

"What should we do?"

Jehu then voiced the question which all of them were thinking. "Will you lead us, Deborah?"

I leaped to my feet. "No!" I shouted. "Deborah will not lead anyone into battle. That's men's work. Do you want a woman to fight your wars for you?"

"But Beriah," shouted Jehu. "She is Israel's shaphat. Yahweh has given her that wisdom and appointed her. To whom else can we turn?"

I clenched my fists. "Jehu," I muttered between clenched teeth, "would you want your wife to fight in battle?"

The crowd grew silent for a brief moment. They understood my feeling, especially when I put it that way. No one would want his own wife to become a warrior.

Jehu, who seemed to be the spokesman for them all, then asked the logical question.

"Tell us, shaphat of Israel. What should we do?"

Again the crowd silenced and looked toward Deborah. She bit her lip. She glanced quickly at me, her eyes pleading. I still stood before her, the chair forgotten. She was the only one seated. I glared at her. She knew how I felt.

Finally she spoke. "Israel needs a leader. My . . . my husband says it is not proper for a woman to go to war. You can understand that, can't you? He does not want his wife to fight in a battle. But someone needs to lead Israel. Who shall it be?"

Amittai, the quiet Zebulonite, spoke for the crowd this time. "God's wisdom is upon you, Deborah *asha* Beriah. You tell us. Who shall be Israel's leader?"

I half expected Deborah to appoint Amittai. Perhaps that's what he had in mind also. I knew he had ideas of revenge in his heart, and I wondered if this prompted him to demand from Israel's shaphat an immediate nomination for the commander of Israel's armies.

I saw Deborah frown briefly. Then she smiled, as though she suddenly knew whom to appoint. The silence in the courtyard was complete now, as we waited her decision.

"Israel's leader," she said slowly, "shall be Barak ben Ahinoam of Naphtali."

We were all silent as we digested this. It was a good selection. Everyone knew about Barak. He lived in Kedesh, not far from Hazor where King Jabin ruled. He had successfully defended his home and city from the Canaanites. He had even gathered a small army around him. A wise choice.

"Will he accept?" I asked.

Jehu spoke. "He will, if he is asked by Israel's shaphat. Will you go to him, Deborah?"

Before Deborah could answer him, I interrupted. "No. I don't want Deborah to travel to Kedesh. The roads are too dangerous. You don't want to endanger the shaphat of Israel, do you?" I could just as easily have said, "endanger my wife," which is what I really meant. But this way of stating it had more impact.

"But —" Jehu looked around. "Who else has the authority to ask Barak? He won't accept the leadership of Israel's army from any of us."

"Yes, he will." Deborah's small voice drew all attention to her. "There is one person he will listen to. Beriah. Because you will speak for me."

The men around us nodded, smiling.

"Yes, yes. She's right."

"You must go to him, Beriah."

"He'll listen to you."

"You speak for Israel's shaphat."

They were right, and I knew it. There was no other way to persuade Barak to send out a call to arms all over Israel. People would respond to him, because Israel's shaphat had asked him to lead them.

"All right," I said. "I'll go. I'll leave tomorrow."

Cheers broke out from the crowd. They were relieved, I'm sure, that decisions had been made and a plan of action adopted. I could see the relief on their faces. My own face probably reflected the same relief.

Deborah had not finished. "Each of you must pledge to Barak your support. Assign as many warriors to him as you can spare. Let no one shirk his duty."

She was right again. Barak could not be persuaded to accept leadership unless he knew we were all behind him.

I decided to be the first to make a pledge. "I will furnish seventy-seven warriors," I said loudly. "They will be led by Nubt-Re, a trained mercenary. They will be armed and equipped with provisions until the *yoreh*."

My offer to provide a small army until the beginning of the next rainy season was the spark needed to ignite the fire.

"I can pledge him forty-nine men," shouted Jehu.

"And I twenty-eight," offered Ashvath.

Amittai stepped forward. "I'll return to Zebulon and recruit all the survivors of Harosheth and Gath-Hepher I can find. We'll be in Kedesh as soon as the rainy season is done."

Others spoke up. Every man there pledged what he could. This was not just patriotic emotion of the moment. It was fear. The situation was desperate, and every Israelite here knew it. We would be fighting for survival.

Just then Zimri came puffing up to Deborah with her lyre. She took it, giving him a grateful smile. The men of Israel in the courtyard again became silent as she plucked its strings.

She sang. "Yahweh is my strength, my song, my salvation. He is my God; I will praise him."

Miriam's song. The same song she had sung yesterday, which had such a stunning effect on me and our guests. Now it had the same effect. She reminded us in clear soprano notes that Yahweh was the strength and salvation of our forefathers. It was he who brought us out of the land of Egypt. It was he who rolled the waters back and destroyed our enemies.

An old song, well known to every one of

us, the most thrilling song an Israelite could possibly hear. It worked its miracle now, far better than any words Deborah could have spoken.

"All the people of Canaan melt with fear," she sang. "Your people, whom you redeemed, will pass by safely. You will bring them in, plant them on your holy mountain. Yahweh, you will provide a sanctuary for them."

And finally, with a loud chord, she concluded her song. "Sing to Yahweh, for he has triumphed gloriously; the horse and its rider he has thrown into the sea! Yahweh will reign for ever and ever!"

As the final note hung in the silence of the courtyard, all of us knew we could do it. The God who brought us safely out of slavery in Egypt was still with us. We could march off to war now. We were not alone.

Yahweh was with us. The horse and its rider would once again be thrown into the sea!

18

The next morning, I talked to Nubt-Re about going with me to Kedesh to speak to Barak.

"How many men will we need to be safe on the roads?" I asked him.

"Just you and me," he replied. "We go at night. Ride donkey. Canaanites, they sleep at night. We go fast. Spend one day at Shechem, then next night ride to Kedesh."

His plan seemed sensible to me, so that night, mounted on donkeys, we left Bethel. The sturdy beasts were sure-footed and swift, and before dawn we arrived at the gates of my father-in-law's house. Nubt-Re was right; no Canaanites were abroad in the dark.

Becher was glad to see us, and when he heard of our mission, he pledged a large army of his own to serve with Barak. We spent the day resting, then that night we set out for the last leg of our journey.

Again we encountered no Canaanites. We arrived at Kedesh shortly after dawn. The Kedesh gate was manned by alert guards who challenged us and demanded our business. When we told them who we were, they let us in.

"Where will I find Barak ben Ahinoam?" I asked the guard at the gate.

"In the house." He pointed toward the only house in town. "He's meeting with his captains."

So . . . Barak was an early riser and had called a meeting of his captains early in the morning. It told me something about him.

As we walked toward the house, I looked at the town. It was more a military camp than a city. The wall was mostly breastwork, with sharpened logs pointing outward about the height of a horse's breast. Very effective against a chariot attack. I mentioned this to Nubt-Re, but he only grunted and offered no opinion.

The tents in the village were not permanent, although women and children were living in them. Barak's house seemed lonely and out of place in this tent-camp.

The man who greeted us at the door was tall and thin, almost cadaverous. His sunken eyes and hollow cheeks made his head look like a skull. The gray hair was straight and sparse on top. His gray beard was short and straight. I judged him to be old, probably in his fifties.

"Welcome, strangers." He spoke in a strong bass voice. "My house is yours. My servants are yours. You are welcome to stay for two nights and the day between."

"Yahweh bless you, Barak ben Ahinoam," I said. "I thank you for your hospitality. I am Beriah ben Jonathan of Ephraim. I have come from Bethel to see you."

"You are most welcome. Everyone has heard of the husband of Israel's shaphat. Please come into my house. Before we talk, I shall have my servant wash your feet and bring you refreshments. My captains and I are going over our assignments for the day —"

I gasped and clutched his arm. Inside the house — a typical four-room house with four stone pillars dividing the large main room — the captains had gathered. Four of them.

And one of them was Heber the Kenite.

Heber had aged since I last saw him at my wedding in Shechem. His hair was white, and he had lost all his teeth, giving him a skeletal look. He had grown fat.

I felt my face growing hot and my jaw tightening. The old hatred surged through me, boiling like a caldron of water on a fire. Images flooded my mind, images of the body of my brother Rakem being carried by his son Modan toward the gates of Shechem, of my standing over his body and lifting my voice in a sacred vow of blood revenge against his murderer.

Heber.

He was as surprised to see me as I to see him. At first he frowned. His mouth opened, revealing one lone rotten tooth. He recovered quickly and grinned.

"Well. Beriah. We meet again. I heard you swore a blood revenge against me. Hah? Is that so?"

I stared at him, unable to say anything.

"How's your wife, Beriah? The lovely Deborah. The shaphat of Israel now. Hah! Don't be so touchy, Beriah. Just because I killed your no-good brother in a fair fight —"

"Heber!" Barak's sharp word brought the old Kenite's mockery to an abrupt end. "Beriah ben Jonathan is a guest in my house. He will be treated as such."

"All right," grumbled Heber. "I respect the laws of hospitality. But any time you want to fulfill your vow of vengeance, we'll go outside this house, outside this city, and we'll settle it. Hah? You want to do it now, Beriah? Or does that make your knees turn to water? You can't —"

"That's enough!" The iron in Barak's voice startled me. Here was a man who demanded respect, even from an uncouth independent boor like Heber.

I took a deep breath, struggling to control myself, and turned away from Heber to face my host. "What — what's he doing here? Is he one of your captains?"

Barak nodded, studying me from beneath his craggy brows. "Heber," he said, his eyes not leaving my face. "Take a seat at the other end of the room. Beriah, sit here beside me."

I sat on the carpet beside him. So did Nubt-Re. A servant brought us drink, cheese, and bread, then began to wash our feet.

I sat with my back to Heber and tried to shut him out of my mind. My business with Barak was more important than my quarrel with the Kenite.

"Now," said Barak, his voice soft and deliberate. "Why have you come to me, Beriah ben Jonathan?"

I forced myself to concentrate, knowing that behind me Heber stared at my back.

"I bring you greetings from the shaphat of Israel. She would have come herself, but the roads were too dangerous."

He nodded. This statement needed no elaboration. I continued. "The message I bring you from the shaphat of Israel is this: 'Thus says Yahweh: The time has come to smite the Canaanites with the sword. Behold, I have summoned the son of Ahinoam to lead my people Israel against them.' "

The wording of my statement had been carefully thought out ahead of time. It was customary for a person in authority to claim that he spoke for God. All the shaphats had done it in the past. Barak would know that this was an official word from Israel's shaphat.

Barak sat silently on the carpet before me. As I looked at his thin face and dark eyes under craggy brows, I wondered if my message came as a surprise to him. If it did, he gave no indication.

When he finally spoke, his guttural voice was resonant. "Am I Israel's shaphat? No. Deborah is the one whom Yahweh has raised up to lead his people."

"Deborah is Israel's judicial shaphat," I replied. "But not the military shaphat. That's why Yahweh now calls the son of Ahinoam."

"If I sound the trumpet," he said, using the ancient phrase to describe the mobilization of Israel, "the people will not respond. They will not go into battle with me as their leader. They will follow no one but Israel's shaphat."

"You know very well that a woman cannot lead an army into battle." I decided to use the tactic which had worked so well before. "Would you like it if your wife were asked to fight your wars for you?"

"I have no wife," he said brusquely.

For a silent moment, we glared at each other. Finally I spoke. "Should we risk the shaphat of Israel in battle?"

"Yahweh will be her shield and buckler," he countered.

"No." My voice came out almost as guttural as his. "I will not permit my wife to fight."

"And I," he said firmly, "will not sound the trumpet in Israel unless Deborah stands beside me."

We continued to glare at each other. The room was filled with a tense silence. I sensed the iron in him. Nothing would move him. Perhaps he sensed the same in me.

It was Barak who broke the silence. "Why don't we ask the shaphat of Israel? She is the one to whom Yahweh has given wisdom. Ask her, Beriah ben Jonathan, if Yahweh has commanded her to take up arms and stand beside me in battle."

"And if she says no?"

He sighed, and I could detect a softness in his iron voice. "If she says no, then the son of Ahinoam will stand alone in the battle. For that is the will of Yahweh."

I rose to my feet, thinking I had won a small victory. Deborah was an obedient wife. She would do as I commanded her.

"I shall go to her immediately," I said. "Nubt-Re and I will leave tonight."

Barak stood. "You must rest now. Sleep in the tent of one of my captains."

His mention of his captains reminded me I was still in the presence of my enemy. "Thank you, Barak ben Ahinoam. I shall accept your hospitality, but I will not sleep in the tent of the Kenite."

He nodded and walked with me toward the door of the house. "What is it between you and Heber, Beriah?"

"He killed my brother. I have sworn blood revenge against him."

"I see." He stroked his short gray beard. "That is between you and him, but it will have to wait until after the war with the Canaanites. May I count on that?"

I nodded. "It has waited this long. Perhaps Yahweh will kill him in battle. If not, I will do it myself. But not, I promise, until there is peace in the land."

"God go with you, Beriah ben Jonathan."

"And with you, Barak ben Ahinoam."

Barak's servant led us to a tent where we slept without being disturbed through the day. In the late afternoon I awoke. Nubt-Re wasn't in the tent. I stepped outside, wondering where he had gone. I didn't have far to look. He was talking with a warrior who was standing guard on the top of the breast-works.

He saw me looking for him, stepped down, and walked toward me. His shaven face was sober. I asked him what was the matter.

"Kedesh not safe," he muttered.

"What do you mean?"

"Smart general, like Sisera, he know how to take it."

He went on, describing in technical terms how the town could be easily captured by any military man who knew enough about siege and warfare. I frowned, not liking what I was hearing. I trusted Nubt-Re's judgment in military matters. I had seen him in action and knew personally of his competence. More than that, he had come highly recommended from Egypt, where he had been a rising officer of great promise in the Egyptian army. Why he left Egypt was a mystery, but as long as he did his job efficiently, I didn't care.

I trusted his judgment about the vulnerability of Kedesh. If that were so, then what did that say about the military competence of Barak?

"What would you suggest?" I asked Nubt-Re.

He grinned. "Move," he replied. "Move very fast."

Maybe he thought that was funny, but I didn't. "Where?" I demanded.

The grin left his face as he saw I was serious. "Only one place I know safe. That Mount Tabor."

"Mount Tabor? Why there?"

Once again he launched into a technical discussion of military tactics, but I cut him short. "We must leave soon. Look, the sky is already darkening."

He nodded. "I go get donkeys ready."

He went to the gate where the donkeys were kept, while I went to say good-bye to Barak.

We left Kedesh at sundown, stopped again at Shechem where we spent the day, then completed our trip the next night. When daylight came, we were still several miles from home. Fortunately we met a group of about twenty armed Israelites traveling to Bethel. Their leader, a wealthy man from the tribe of Asher, was seeking judgment from Deborah.

I went directly to Deborah's palm tree, where I knew she would be holding court. Deborah received me warmly, although she expressed concern about my making such a dangerous trip.

I pointed to the donkey I had ridden and said, "You have him to thank for my safety, my dear. He may look like a donkey, but he's really an eagle. We flew from Kedesh in two nights and saw no Canaanites, since they were earthbound."

She laughed, and put her hand on the ass's head. "Thank you, *nesher*, for taking care of my beloved. Your wings are indeed swift."

The donkey, perhaps wondering why Deborah called him an eagle, snorted and tossed his head.

"I bring a message from Barak," I said.

She immediately sobered and turned away from the donkey. "Tell me here, Beriah. This concerns everyone."

I looked around. The usual group of petitioners had gathered, men from all over Israel. Their guards had been scattered up and down the road to mingle with my own.

Deborah was right. The message I brought to her from Barak did concern them. It concerned all Israel.

Through the long nights while riding on the donkey, I had thought over what I should say to Deborah. I knew I must report to her Barak's conditional acceptance. But I knew also that I must present my own strong statement — the command of a husband to his wife — that she must disregard Barak's condition.

I raised my voice so that everyone present

could hear. I also used formal language. "Hear the word of Barak ben Ahinoam, whom Yahweh has raised up to be the military shaphat of Israel. I will accept the command of the army of Yahweh, but only on the condition that Deborah, the political shaphat of Israel, stand by my side in the battle."

Although I kept my eyes on Deborah, I heard a gasp from the assembled men. They knew as well as I that a woman had no place on the battlefield. They would know also how I, her husband, would feel about it.

When I spoke next, my voice was as hard as I could make it. "Thus says Beriah ben Jonathan, husband of Israel's shaphat: I will not permit my beloved to take up arms and fight for Israel. I, her husband, have spoken."

Again, I heard the gasp from the men around us. They would know what was happening here. They could feel the strain between us — husband and wife — and the depth of emotion which flowed between us in that moment. They waited for Deborah's answer.

She had been looking at me, listening intently until that moment. Then she lowered her eyes and bowed her head. Her shoulders slumped slightly. I could see tears rolling from the corners of her eyes. For a long moment she stood like that. A long moment in which the silence stretched out. No one spoke. We all waited for Deborah.

When she finally spoke, her voice was frail. She said the words without raising her eyes to look at me. "I must choose between the will of Yahweh and the will of my husband."

I knew then what was coming, but I was powerless to prevent it.

What she said next was barely above a whisper. "Thus says Yahweh through the shaphat whom he has appointed: Behold, Barak and Deborah shall stand side by side in the battle, and together they shall drive out the forces of Jabin and Sisera. Yahweh has spoken."

I stood there, staring at her. What could I say? Yahweh had spoken. Whether this was the actual will of Yahweh or not, I had no way of knowing. The formal language only meant this was Deborah's way of saying what she believed to be God's will. But she was Israel's divinely appointed shaphat, and the wisdom of Yahweh was upon her. I could not change the decree from God. It superseded the will of the husband.

Then Deborah raised her eyes and looked at me. I saw such anguish in them that I could not be angry with her. She was devastated by her decision. By God's decision. She had to obey God, not me. It wasn't her fault. It was Yahweh's.

I went to her then, and put my arms around her. She sobbed into my shoulder. I was the only one who could hear her as she whispered, "Oh Beriah! Beriah! I'm so sorry."

Yahweh had done this to us!

The benevolent deity who enters the lives of his people, giving them his love and kindness, his individual attention, protecting them, guiding them, helping them in all aspects of life — this was the God who was now sending my wife into battle, risking her life.

I kissed her gently on the top of her head, then lifted my eyes toward the heavens. I wanted in that moment to curse Yahweh forever. But I could not. Everything in my life, my family background, the ancient traditions and beliefs of my people, prevented me. I was an Israelite. I could not curse God.

"All right," I whispered to her. "You may stand with Barak on the field of battle. But I will stand beside you. If you die, we will both die. Together."

19

That night at bedtime, I finally had an opportunity to speak with Deborah alone. We were both exhausted — Deborah from her hard day in the judgment seat, and I from my tiring trip, followed by the many duties I had to catch up on which awaited my arrival.

I told her what Nubt-Re had said about Kedesh's vulnerability to attack by an intelligent general. This disturbed her as much as it did me, since it raised questions about Barak's competence as a military strategist.

"Whom do you believe?" she asked me.

"Nubt-Re," I replied without hesitation. I reviewed for her his qualifications and recommendations. She agreed. Part of her wisdom was knowing whose advice to follow.

"What should we do?" I asked. "Replace Barak with Nubt-Re as commander-in-chief of Israel?"

"No," she said. "Barak would not agree to that, nor would the men of Israel. Nubt-Re is, after all, an Egyptian."

"Then, I suppose, you will have to order

Barak to follow Nubt-Re's advice on military strategy."

She frowned. "No. There is only one way to make this work. I must stand between them. I will listen to Nubt-Re as he outlines the strategy, then I will tell Barak what to do."

I nodded. That would work. Deborah was Israel's shaphat, and Barak — and all Israel, for that matter — knew that God's wisdom was upon her. If Deborah said, "Thus says Yahweh," no one would question that Yahweh had spoken to her. And if Deborah proposed military strategy, that too would be accepted without question.

The next night we sent a messenger on a swift donkey to Kedesh, telling Barak to sound the trumpet in Naphtali and Zebulon and assemble at Mount Tabor before the yoreh, the first rain. We sent several messengers to all the other tribes of Israel, asking them to mobilize their warriors and send them to us before the yoreh.

Then we began our own plans.

I had pledged seventy-seven warriors. I already had forty-nine in my employ, trained by Nubt-Re and skilled not only in spear and swordsmanship but also in the bow and arrow. When I spread the word among the shepherds and farmers that we needed more men to fight the Canaanites, many responded. They were mostly youths, bored with farming and herding and dull routine, wanting the glamour of war.

I raised more than my pledge of seventy-seven warriors. I needed them all, however. To maintain an army in the field takes a lot of behind-the-scenes activity. The army must be supplied with grain and meat. To do that, the farming and herding must be carried out. And the workers must be guarded. When I left my nephew Modan behind to supervise my estate, I charged him to send us a constant supply of food.

About a month before the yoreh, we set out for Mount Tabor. By that time we had a very large army — not only my seventy-seven, but also more than a hundred from my neighbors. The tribe of Ephraim would be well represented.

We stopped at Shechem to visit Deborah's father. Becher was glad to see us. He had not seen Deborah since our marriage, almost twenty years before. He also had the largest army from Ephraim ready to march to Mount Tabor with us, commanded by Becher's son-in-law, Ezer.

Ezer was a few years older than I, and I was impressed by his no-nonsense approach to his responsibilities. His first statement to us was to place his entire command at the disposal of Deborah. Altogether we made up a contingent of more than four hundred men.

As we marched toward Mount Tabor — safely, because of our numbers — we saw no Canaanites. I suspected Sisera and Jabin knew all about our mobilization and were collecting an army of their own. Rumors reached us that they were gathering at Harosheth, which meant Sisera was in charge. We had heard of his cleverness and military expertise. The war ahead of us would not be easy.

We arrived at Mount Tabor on a clear day, shortly before sunset. Although I had seen the mountain before, I studied it now from a military perspective.

Mount Tabor looks like a large inverted bowl on the northern part of the Valley of Jezreel. It is almost perfectly round, with the steepest parts at its base. Although heavily forested, the top gives a commanding view of the entire plain below. No chariot could mount its incline, and armed men on foot would have to fight their way uphill.

Nubt-Re joined me as we gazed at our home for the next few weeks. "Barak, he already here," muttered Nubt-Re. "See?"

He pointed to the top, where we could make out some activity. If there were men occupying the slopes, we could not see them for the trees.

"Then he did come," said Deborah, who had just joined us.

"Are you surprised?" I asked. "Who would disobey a summons from the shaphat of Israel?"

She shrugged, saying nothing. But it made me wonder — how many in Israel felt that way about their shaphat? How many tribes would respond to Deborah's call to arms?

We saw something else as we approached the mountain: Canaanites. Groups of armed men roamed the broad plain, but they were too few and too disorganized to attack such a strong force as ours. Nubt-Re did, however, order the flocks and herds, which we had brought with us for a fresh food supply, to be drawn closer to the main body of men.

At the slopes of Mount Tabor we immediately faced a problem. With at least three weeks before the yoreh, the mountain was already inhabited by several thousand warriors from Naphtali and Zebulon. Where should we quarter our men and supplies? I suggested the Hill of Moreh, which was closest to Mount Tabor. But Nubt-Re said it was indefensible. He chose Mount Gilboa, a little farther away, but more easily defended. Deborah concurred.

Nubt-Re began to issue orders, but at a word from Deborah, he stopped. "Let Ezer do it," she said. "You come with us."

Deborah's quick wisdom never ceased to amaze me. This was a monumental task, and Ezer, her brother-in-law from Shechem, was probably the most capable person among us to handle it. Nubt-Re was a master of military tactics; that was why Deborah wanted him with us as we climbed to the top of the mountain to meet with Barak.

Mount Tabor was steeper than it looked from the Plain of Jezreel. We were winded when we reached the top. There the mountain rounded off onto a flat mesa, with not as many trees as on the slopes.

Barak came forward to greet us. I was surprised at how much older he looked. Perhaps away from his home, the responsibility of commander of Israel's forces weighed heavily upon him. His gray hair was even more stringy and sparse, and his gaunt features seemed even leaner. His straight beard hung limply on his face.

But he was smiling as he came toward us.

"Deborah, shaphat of Israel," he said warmly. That he greeted her first before Nubt-Re and me was an indication of his respect for the shaphat, even though she was a woman.

"Barak, commander-in-chief of the forces of Israel," she replied, just as formally. It was a complimentary title. Everyone in Israel knew Deborah was the actual commander-in-chief, and Barak titular commander only. But it was a gracious compliment, and Barak gratefully accepted it.

Barak led us to his camp, situated on the center of the mountaintop. It seemed comfortable enough. There was a large tent — far larger than one man needed, but undoubtedly used for staff councils during the rainy season. There were also several benches and a table outside near the cooking ovens. Other commanders had their own smaller tents pitched near by. He pointed out the tent which he had reserved for Deborah and me. Nubt-Re would have to fend for himself.

In spite of the rustic nature of the small village, Barak offered us hospitality. A servant brought refreshments, placing them on the table outside. The servant then knelt before us and washed our feet. He began with Deborah, another surprise. Had it ever happened before in Israel, that a man — even though a servant — washed a woman's feet?

Never, as long as I shall live, will I forget the opening words of our conference as we sat there at the table on the top of Mount Tabor.

"Deborah, shaphat of Israel," Barak began,

using the formal title. "Now that you're here, victory will soon be ours."

"Barak, commander-in-chief of Israel." Deborah looked solemnly into his eyes. "Surely you must be aware that by inviting me here, the credit for the defeat of Sisera and the Canaanites will always be given to a woman, rather than to you."

At the time she said these words, none of us knew how prophetic they would be. Nor that the woman she referred to would not be Deborah.

Barak nodded, his voice as solemn as Deborah's. "So be it. Let the glory be given to Yahweh."

I nodded approvingly. A pious statement, even if Barak was not a particularly pious man. What I thought he really meant was, "It doesn't matter who gets the credit, as long as the job gets done." This kind of humility was rare in a man. But it was necessary if there were to be no friction at the top of command. How easily Barak could have been jealous of Deborah.

Barak, I concluded, was the ideal commander for Israel. He was not experienced in military tactics, but he was willing to take orders from Deborah, who would be well versed in military strategy with Nubt-Re at her side.

Barak's strongest point was his ability to command men. They would follow him into battle, especially when they knew that the plans were formulated by Deborah, who, for all they knew, had received them from God himself.

And maybe she had.

I pulled on my beard as I watched the three people before me who were the leaders of this campaign. If anyone could bring us success — against large numbers of professional Canaanite soldiers and chariots — it would be these three. Deborah's wisdom had brought them together. And Deborah's wisdom came from God.

20

The days seemed to pass slowly. We settled in to wait for the yoreh, when we would finally be called to fight. Meanwhile we waited.

We watched from the top of Mount Tabor as the Canaanite chariots roamed the Valley of Jezreel. They were everywhere, flaunting their strength. Sometimes we counted them in the hundreds.

Everyone seemed to accept Deborah's proclamation that we would not attack during the dry season. Even I, with little military knowledge, saw the wisdom in this. We would stand little chance against the superior forces of the Canaanites, with their well-trained soldiers. And their chariots, on dry ground, would slaughter us.

Even so the men on Mount Tabor were restless, wanting to fight. Or perhaps they just wanted to get it over with and go home. They had left behind their families and farms. Sheep needed sheared and crops must be planted or harvested. By now, the time of the grape harvest, the men were especially impatient and edgy. This was a time when families normally relaxed and celebrated the joy of living.

Water became a problem. There was no source of water on Mount Tabor, and we had to send groups of men out at night to bring in water from the plain. The Canaanites soon discerned our forays, and they attacked our water squads. We learned to send the squads during the darkest part of the night. What worked best was not a large armed force to guard them, but a small, fast contingent which would move in, load the asses with jugs of water, then run. Even so we lost a lot of men during these water forays. But we had to do it or perish of thirst.

Occasionally I glimpsed Heber the Kenite among the captains. I never spoke to him, and he seemed to go out of his way to avoid me. Maybe it was because Deborah was always with me. Or maybe it was because of his highly developed respect for the laws of hospitality. We were, after all, guests of Barak on this mountain.

One of the captains, however, I was glad to see — Amittai ben Shelesh. True to his promise, he had returned to Zebulon and recruited all the surviving men who had suf-

at the hands of Sisera. They repre-
d a large force of determined men with
to fight for.

Nubt-Re showed his versatility during these long months of waiting. He was made welcome at the captains' tents, as they began to appreciate his knowledge and skill in the military arts. He convinced them of the need to become bowmen as well as spearmen. Soon he had set up an archery range on top of the mountain. Not only the captains, but also many of the warriors gathered there to learn the art of archery. His standard message was, "When fighting chariots, kill horses first. Then fight the men."

During the long days and nights of the last few weeks of the dry season, we kept in touch with Ezer on Mount Gilboa. He was having an easier time than we, mainly because of the location. He was closer to a water supply and also to home. Men from our company of Ephraimites often left for a day or two to go home. We could not do that on Mount Tabor, which was too isolated. At the time I questioned Nubt-Re's choice of this mountain for central headquarters, but I learned later that this was the best place to strike against the enemy.

We also learned from Ezer that more recruits were coming in all the time. A large force from Manassah had arrived and placed themselves under Ezer's command. A smaller group from Benjamin joined them, but we noticed that the more remote tribes, such as Reuben, Gad, and Dan, were missing. I wondered too what had happened to Jehu and his promise of a large levy of forces from Judah. I asked Deborah about this.

She shrugged. "Perhaps they are too far away. After all, they have not been bothered by the Canaanites like we have."

"But are we not Israel? Or are we just a group of independent tribes?"

She smiled. "We are both, I think. I don't have the same authority as a king, to demand their obedience."

"Maybe you should," I replied. "Maybe what Israel needs is a king. Then in times of crisis like this, obedience could be demanded, not requested."

"No!" Deborah's vehemence surprised me. "Israel's king is Yahweh. He is our strength. Let Yahweh raise up a shaphat when necessary. But we want no kings."

"No, not if they would act like the petty kings around us here in the land of Canaan. They're arrogant, weak, and stupid. But if our king were a deeply religious person, we would still have a nation ruled by God, but united."

She shrugged. "Maybe a kingdom will come some day in Israel. But if so it will mean the end of the time when Yahweh rules Israel through a shaphat. But a king, and the line of kings which would come from him, would be subject to arrogance, temptation, and eventually corruption. That's a big price to pay for instant obedience in time of war."

That was not our immediate problem, however. We faced a difficult concern now: morale. With the occasional night skirmishes by our water patrols, and with increasing inactivity, our people wanted to fight. But they could not, until the rainy season was upon us.

Deborah then began to visit the troops. She would go from one group to another with her lyre and sing to them. Wherever we went, they welcomed us, and listened attentively to her words of encouragement and her songs.

Although at first the favorite song was the song of Miriam, she began to sing another song which became quite popular. I have to admit the words were mine, one of my "empty" poems which I composed for the occasion. She put it to a martial tune, and the men of Israel loved it.

Praise Yahweh!
The sons of Israel were determined to fight;
The people of the Promise gladly volunteered.
Listen to me, O kings and princes,
Pay attention to me, you rulers.
For I sing about Yahweh,
The God of Israel.

I could feel the pent-up excitement of the men as they listened to her. They stood around, grasping their spears, wishing for battle. With Deborah as their leader, they believed themselves invincible.

How I rejoice in the commanders of Israel,
With the strong people who gladly
    volunteered!
The village musicians will gather at the well,
To sing the triumphs of the people of Yahweh!

I had mixed feelings about how much good this song did for the morale of our men. On the one hand, it contributed to their restlessness, their impatience, their eagerness to fight, even before the right time came. On the other hand, it helped their mood remain cheerful and confident, rather than depressed and complaining. Wherever Deborah went, the people cheered her, and no one grumbled.

As we moved among the men of Israel, we heard many things, although two impressions remain with me through the years. One was what they called Deborah. Not shaphat, Israel's judge, who mediated their disputes and now led them into battle. Now they called her by a different name, one I thought very appropriate — Mother. An apt description. "Mother" was a term of respect. Even though she had no children, Deborah seemed to have adopted Israel, making all Israelites her children.

The other impression was what they called me. You would think they would have known me by now. I was Beriah ben Jonathan, direct descendant of Ephraim ben Joseph. I was a leading landowner in Israel.

But what they called me now was Eshet Lappidoth, the spouse of a spirit-filled woman.

Perhaps that was only just. God had not called me for anything special. No, God had just called me to be the husband and provider for Israel's Mother. But I was not thereby Israel's Father. I was Eshet Lappidoth. A nobody.

I accepted my role meekly. Around me, men were preparing to fight for Israel. Perhaps to die for Israel. While I — I waited only to stand beside Israel's Mother.

And so we all waited. We waited while below us on the Plain of Jezreel Sisera's chariots paraded daily, offering challenges, calling us cowards, daring us to come out and fight. We waited while our numbers were depleted by our nightly forays for water. We waited through the heat and dryness of the days and the contrasting coolness of the nights. We waited.

Day after agonizingly slow day, we waited. The yoreh, the first rain of the season, crept closer. The men looked at gathering clouds. Any day now. It would come.

Then we could fight.

21

When the yoreh finally came, it arrived with a large downpour. The evening was hot, airless, and humid. As darkness fell, large drops splattered in the dust and rustled the leaves of the trees. Then suddenly it was upon us, a deluge of hard, driving rain.

Darkness came with the rain. Almost immediately after sunset, the mountain was plunged into a dungeon-like blackness surrounded by a wall of noise, the din of hard falling rain.

We had already made our plans. Each captain knew his assigned position, and each warrior knew whom he was to follow. Ezer on Mount Gilboa had his orders, and he would be preparing now to leave. As we were.

In spite of the darkness, the sudden chill, the noise, and the hard-beating rain, there was an excitement among the men. The days of waiting were over.

Barak led us down the mountain and onto the Plain of Jezreel. Deborah and I stayed near him; I noticed Nubt-Re was not far behind. We could hear the captains shouting orders. Yes, shouting. The rain was so loud they had to shout to be heard.

We marched across the valley toward the Kishon River. We arrived at its swollen banks about sunrise and quickly crossed. The tiny stream was now a raging torrent, waist-high. Nubt-Re and I held Deborah; we would not want to lose her before the battle started.

The captains led their men to the assigned positions just below the two Canaanite towns of Taanach and Megiddo. We hoped the townspeople could see us through the driving rain, so they would report our presence to Sisera.

We waited through the morning, our battle lines drawn. It wasn't an easy wait. We were cold and wet. Beneath our feet the mud seemed ankle deep.

I began to doubt the plan of battle would work. Sisera was no fool; he wouldn't come out to challenge us in this weather. He would wait until his chariots found firmer ground, then he would cut us to pieces. Meanwhile he would just leave us standing here, soaked, shivering, until the battle conditions suited him.

I said as much to Deborah. She smiled at

me. "He'll come," she muttered. "Just remember who commands the forces of Israel."

I looked into her rain-soaked face, wondering what she meant. Barak commanded Israel. No, that wasn't exactly correct; Deborah commanded Israel. Deborah. Israel's shaphat, appointed by Yahweh himself.

Then I knew what she meant. Yahweh commanded Israel. Yahweh was the only one who could bring Sisera out.

And come out Sisera did. Word came to us from our scouts that a force of chariots was making their way toward us from the east. Hundreds of them, so they said. And thousands of warriors.

Sisera could not resist the challenge. He had finally drawn out his enemy to face him on the field of battle, and he was not to be denied by a little mud and rain.

The battle plan drawn up by Barak, Deborah, and Nubt-Re called for us to meet the enemy where the Kishon River forks. Two main tributaries came together there beneath Taanach and Megiddo, where they merged into a sizable stream, fed also by the springs of Megiddo. Just a few days before, the riverbed was dry, with only a trickle of water. Now it was not only full, but overflowing. The marshy plain here by the forks was where we had taken our stand.

At that moment, the rain stopped.

At the time, I despaired. We needed the mud to stop the chariots. Had there been enough rain to soak the ground, or was it still firm enough for the horses and wheeled vehicles to maneuver? Caught out in the open like this, we would all be at the mercy of the chariots.

Later I realized what had happened. Too much rain would have been our undoing. Too much mud would have made it impossible even for our troops to maneuver, and we too might have been swept away in the current. The amount of rain was just right. It provided a delicate balance of enough mud to stop the chariots and at the same time enable us to move rapidly around them. Yahweh had provided. But I didn't know that at the time; I thought only of the oncoming chariots.

I had never been in a battle before and didn't know what to expect. I thought it might be a lot of fighting at all times, but it wasn't. Most of the fighting occurred to the west of us. We could hear it, now that the rain had stopped. Shouts. Clash of weapons and armor. Snorting and shrieking of horses. Screams. And terror. Terror seemed to be a tangible thing on the battlefield.

We learned later that our battle plan worked. Our archers, trained by Nubt-Re, killed the horses. They were easy targets, as they stood fetlock-deep in the mud, struggling to move. Then we attacked the charioteers. The entire corps of several hundred chariots were rendered ineffective. The first round of the battle belonged to us.

But we still faced their army, and they were trained soldiers. Our men were shepherds and farmers, family men who had been called out for this occasion. We faced professionals, who spent their lives preparing for battle.

That was when the battle began in earnest. Barak and Nubt-Re went to join the front ranks, while Deborah and I stayed behind. A small squad of warriors stayed to guard us. We could dimly see the battle and could hear it, but we were ignorant of the actual progress. And we were frightened.

I looked at Deborah. Her clothes were soaking wet; she was shivering. Her face was white. Her mouth was set in a tight line. When she saw me looking at her, she managed a brave smile. But the small wrinkles around her eyes told me she was as frightened as I was.

The battle surged closer to us. We could

now see some of the isolated incidents. A spear fight occurred not fifty paces from us, between an Israelite and a Canaanite. The Canaanite had the greater skill, and he thrust his spear into his opponent's arm. The youth slipped in the muddy soil and went down, with the Canaanite poised just above him to deliver the final deadly blow. Then two other Israelites attacked him.

We saw several such incidents, each one it seemed a little closer. One body of Canaanites seemed determined to press on toward where we stood. They may have known that the shaphat of Israel was here, as they kept pointing toward us and shouting. They were succeeding, too, coming closer.

Would this, then, be the destruction of Israel's hopes? Would our lives end here on this muddy plain? I gripped my spear tightly. A long time ago, I had taken training in spear fighting, but I was always awkward and ineffective, and since then I had had no practice. So be it. I would die here. But I would fight, and be the first to die. I couldn't bear to see Deborah killed before my eyes.

They were coming closer, shouting, wielding their spears and swords efficiently, mowing down our guards as they tried to stand on the slippery ground. In a few minutes, it would be all over.

Then suddenly, from our right, a shout arose and a new group of men smashed into the fight. They attacked the Canaanites on their flank, driving them to the side. Men in helmets and upper body armor. Kenites.

They were led by Heber.

He was awesome. He wielded a large two-edged sword with both hands, flailing about him with skill and energy. His long white hair whipped around his head. His toothless mouth was open, shouting, although I couldn't make out his words. He seemed never to lose his footing, possibly because he was the aggressor and the Canaanites before him were moving backward. They fell away.

Then suddenly it was over. The battle moved away from us, leaving only the wounded behind. Our surviving guards quickly dispatched them, and we were surprised by the abrupt silence. Far away, it seemed, the battle continued, but here, it was quiet.

Deborah and I stared at each other, hardly daring to believe that we still lived. Then suddenly she came into my arms. I dropped the spear and held her, each of us trembling. We clung to each other for a long time, each trying to give the other strength, trying to control the panic and horror churning within us.

A guttural voice startled us. "Deborah, shaphat of Israel." It was Barak. He, Nubt-Re, and Ezer were walking toward us. Their clothes were muddy and wet, their hair and beards plastered to their fore-heads and faces by either sweat or rain. But they stood before us proudly, their heads held high.

Barak spoke first. "Yahweh has given us the victory. They are running. We have won. Praise Yahweh!"

Deborah and I said nothing. Indeed, we could not have uttered a word in that moment. Horror still gripped us.

"Ezer made the difference," continued Barak. "He and his men arrived from Mount Gilboa just in time to turn the battle in our favor. It couldn't have been timed better, for we were tired and they were fresh."

Other warriors gathered around us. They were cheering. Slowly it began to reach my awareness. The battle was over. And we had won.

Deborah and I still held each other. We seemed to need the comfort of our embrace. Slowly the horror drained out of us.

Deborah recovered first. "Where's Sisera?" she asked.

I watched the faces of Barak and Nubt-Re as they realized the importance of her question. The smiles of triumph left their faces. They stared at her, openmouthed.

"I don't know," said Barak softly.

"I know." Heber the Kenite came striding forward.

"Where?" asked Barak.

"He's running, too, just like all of those dogs. Only he's running that way!" Heber pointed toward the east.

I could sense more than feel the gasp of the men around me. The surviving army of Canaanites had run west, toward their stronghold at Harosheth. If what Heber said was true, Sisera was running in the opposite direction.

"He's heading for Hazor," said Deborah.

Once again her quick wisdom had analyzed the situation, and we could all see now what was happening. Sisera would realize that the battle was lost, his army destroyed, and the avenging Israelite forces completing their destruction of his forces. His only hope of escape lay in reaching Hazor, the stronghold of his ally King Jabin. From there he would be able to reorganize his forces and attack again. All our work today would then be for nothing.

"We must follow him," said Barak.

"Too late," muttered Heber. "He has too big a start."

Barak ran his hand across his forehead. "But we must try."

"Yes." Deborah stepped forward, her terror forgotten, in complete control of her emotions. Now the shaphat of Israel spoke. "Barak, take Heber's Kenites and pursue him. As fast as you can. Nubt-Re and Ezer, take the rest of the men and pursue the Canaanites, even if you have to go all the way to Harosheth. The army must be totally destroyed. Then report to me at the Hill of Moreh."

The men obeyed her, as though they had been following her orders all their lives. To this day I marvel at that. On the battlefield, just after a victory, in a euphoric moment, they took orders from a woman. Amazing!

22

Our guards prepared a tent for us on the Hill of Moreh. From somewhere they procured a brazier, and soon the tent was warm, even steaming. The rain had started again, this time a drizzle, and the Valley of Jezreel was by now a muddy quagmire.

All through the day, reports reached us of the magnitude of our victory. The entire chariot corps of the Canaanites had been destroyed and their army decimated. We bore heavy losses also. There would be wailing and tearing of clothes in many Israelite homes, mingled with the celebrations of our triumph. Such is the paradox of war.

Nubt-Re kept us informed about the progress of the cleanup campaign against the Canaanite army. He had laid siege to Harosheth and expected it to fall in a few days. The destruction of Sisera's army was almost complete.

When we went to bed that night, we had as yet heard nothing from Barak about his pursuit of Sisera. Nor did he report during the next day. I had little hope of Sisera's capture. Hazor was a walled stronghold, difficult to besiege, almost impossible to attack successfully, although it had fallen to Joshua many years before.

While we waited, Deborah and I talked about the battle. We were just beginning to piece together the parts of the conflict we had only briefly glimpsed at the time. The Kishon River was our greatest ally. Where we had taken our stand at the forks, the ground was marshy but firm enough to fight on. Below the forks, especially as it rushed toward the sea, it had become a raging torrent, and no one was able to ford it. The whole Valley of Esdraelon, where Harosheth was located, was flooded. Many of the Canaanite warriors had been drowned.

"Even the stars in their courses fought against Sisera," commented Deborah. A poetic phrase. I decided to use it in the poem I was composing for Deborah's victory song.

"We owe a lot to the strong arm of Yahweh," I said.

Deborah nodded. "His strong arms. I can name several of them: Barak, Ezer, Amittai —"

"And don't forget Nubt-Re," I said. "Maybe I should have special mention of him in the victory song."

She frowned. "Yes. He certainly deserves it. But will Israel accept praise about a foreigner?"

"I don't know. I'll write about him. We'll see if he is remembered in Israel's history."

"If you are going to praise foreigners in our victory song," Deborah said, her face somber, "you should also remember Heber the Kenite. He certainly made a contribution."

I said nothing. She was right, of course. But once again I recalled the picture of my brother Rakem, killed by his hand. And the blood revenge I had sworn.

Almost as though she read my mind, Deborah placed her hand on mine. "He saved our lives, Beriah."

I sighed. "I know. But. . . ."

"But you have sworn a vow to kill him. And now you have mixed feelings about him. Isn't that right?"

I said nothing. I couldn't even look at her.

She continued. "Beriah, the time has come for you to face your burden. You've carried it a long time. Let's talk about it. Shall we?"

Still I said nothing. I was torn between wanting to withdraw from this painful subject, continuing to nurse my bitterness, and talking about it with Deborah.

She would not let it go. "Tell me, my be-loved," she whispered. "Why do you hate him so?"

"He killed my brother."

"In a fair fight."

"Nevertheless, he killed him."

Her hand closed over mine. "Beriah, my love, this is tearing you up inside. Can't you let it go?"

I shook my head. "I have sworn a vow."

"Forget your vow. It was foolish, impulsive. It is not worth destroying your life over."

I finally looked at her. "You can't walk away from a vow sworn before Yahweh. Vows are sacred."

"No they're not."

I stared at her. What she was saying almost amounted to heresy. Everybody knew that a vow, once made, could not be broken. The Commandments forbid it. That would be the same as taking God's name in vain.

"Beriah," she said, and her voice was urgent. "You know the difference between a vow and a covenant."

"Of course. A covenant is a pact, sworn between a man and God. But what does that have to do with —"

"Look at it this way, Beriah. A covenant is a two-way oath between a person and God. Both of them swear to something. A vow is one-sided. Sworn only by the human. If it is foolish, then why couldn't it be broken? God has not placed his approval on it."

"But if it is sworn in God's name —"

"Then God will forgive. We have a loving and compassionate God. He won't hold a mistake against anyone."

I turned away from her. What she said made sense to me, but it turned upside down what I had always believed. I found it difficult to cast off a familiar doctrine and accept new reasoning, no matter how much sense it made.

I decided on a new approach. "Heber will think me a coward."

"Are you a coward, Beriah?"

I didn't answer her. To tell the truth, I didn't know the answer. For all I knew, I might be.

She turned my face toward her. "My love," she said softly, "the man I saw on the battlefield the other day was very brave. He held his spear in front of him and was ready to give his life to save mine. That man was no coward."

Still I said nothing. It was comforting, however, to hear her say she admired me for my courage.

She continued, still speaking softly. "If I know you're not a coward, and if you can accept your own bravery, then what does it matter what Heber thinks?"

I was quiet, digesting this. She was right again. She was always right. God's wisdom was truly upon her.

What did it matter to me what Heber thought? Or anybody else, for that matter? Deborah believed in me. I could believe in myself, my own courage. So what did I care what Heber thought?

"And besides," added Deborah, smiling shyly, "Heber saw you on the battlefield. I don't think he'll ever be able to call you a coward."

"Doesn't matter," I muttered. "But I still won't put him in the victory song. I just can't do that."

She laughed softly, but it wasn't a derisive laugh. "All right. Don't put Heber in. And put Nubt-Re in. Let's see how that goes."

I recall that conversation vividly, because of the ironic way it turned out. The victory song took several months to prepare, changing often as new stanzas were added and others deleted. Eventually Nubt-Re's place in it was taken out; our people just could not countenance a leading role played by an Egyptian in our great victory.

And Heber's place?

It actually became one of the outstanding

features of the song of victory. But that was mainly because of what happened at the very time Deborah and I were discussing him.

On the third day after the battle, Barak arrived at our tent on the Hill of Moreh. "Praise Yahweh!" he exclaimed when we stepped out of the tent. "His strong arm has given us the victory!"

I had noticed before that Barak was fond of using pious phrases. He wasn't a particularly religious man, but you couldn't tell that from his speech. I have observed this many times — deeply spiritual people are usually low key about displaying their personal faith, while a superficially religious person is often volubly pious.

Since it wasn't raining, we chose to entertain him outside. The interior of the tent was not as fresh and sweet-smelling during the rainy season as the outdoors on a sunny day. Indeed, the air seemed alive with vigor and freshness. A cool breeze swept across the small clearing outside our tent. We seated ourselves on benches and looked out over the Valley of Jezreel, on the battle grounds where Yahweh had given us a victory. On a day like this, anybody could be pious.

Deborah herself brought bread, drink,

and cheese for Barak's refreshment. He had come directly to us, and he was visibly tired and hungry. Even so, he seemed animated, his old-looking face wreathed in smiles.

"Sisera is no more," he exclaimed. "Yahweh has struck him down."

"Ah!" I banged my fist on the table. "That is indeed good news. Tell us what happened."

Barak was in no hurry to tell his story. He pulled a chunk of bread off the loaf and shoved it into his mouth. A few crumbs clung to his stringy beard. He chewed noisily.

"Well," he said, licking his fingers, "it all happened at the Oak of Za-anannim." He reached for the wheel of cheese on the table, cut off a large slice, and crammed it all into his mouth. His teeth were stained.

"The Oaks of Za-anannim," I said impatiently. "Where's that?"

"Just a few miles southwest of the Sea of Chinnereth." He wiped his mouth with the back of his hand and cut off another slice of cheese. "That's where Heber lives."

"Heber!" My old enemy. I still hadn't fully accepted the idea that I would not carry out my vow of vengeance. Deborah's wisdom had pointed out the folly of this vow, but full acceptance of her view would come later, after I had let it settle in my mind. I couldn't make changes that quickly.

Barak continued. "The real hero of this story is Jael, Heber's wife. She was on friendly terms with King Jabin. In fact, she boasted that they had entertained the king once in their tent."

Somewhere I had heard that. Some time in the distant past. I couldn't recall the exact way I had heard it.

Barak spoke around a mouthful of cheese. "She was alone in her tent when Sisera came to her. He was tired and hungry. He asked her for hospitality."

I nodded, recalling how Heber had often spoken respectfully about the laws of hospitality.

"So —" Barak sipped from his cup. "Jael invited him in. She even gave him some milk." He chuckled. "She served it in a very pretty bowl."

He was obviously dragging out his story, enjoying the leisurely telling of his tale. I wished he would get on with it.

"And then —" Barak put his cup down hard, spilling a few drops of his drink on the table. "She invited him to lie down on the floor and sleep."

I frowned. No decent woman would do that. Even though Jael must have been very old, since Heber himself was past fifty, she still had no business offering him a bed in her home when she was alone. The laws of hospitality did not go that far.

"That stupid Sisera." Barak poured more of the liquid into his cup. "He asked Jael to stand guard while he slept. He planned to stay the night, then go on to Hazor in the morning."

I had to agree with him. It was a stupid thing to do. But Sisera trusted Jael, for two reasons. Heber's household was friendly with King Jabin, and also the laws of hospitality included sanctuary.

Barak drank deeply. We waited until he was ready to continue. "Now comes the best part." He grinned. "While he was sleeping, Jael picked up a tent peg and hammer and drove the peg through his temple, pinning him to the ground. Yahweh be praised!"

I shuddered. So did Deborah. Her face was white and her lips were pressed tightly together. Why had Jael done this? She and Heber boasted about their respect for the laws of hospitality. Did she see an opportunity to become the star of Israel's victory?

Barak's grin broadened. "That's how we found him. May all Yahweh's enemies perish that way!"

Absurdly, the first thought that came to me as I pictured this grisly scene was that I would never describe it in the victory song I was composing. It was too horrible. Yahweh didn't do things that way. Somehow I would find a way to tell the story in nobler fashion.

In fact, the story I planned to tell in the victory song would honor Deborah, not Jael. I would never mention Jael. Nor Heber. Never. Neither of them was worthy of a place in the great anthem which would be sung by all the people of Israel. The song would be taught to their children and their children's children. It would be a noble song, praising Yahweh, honoring Deborah, enshrining our magnificent victory in the memories of our people.

But never — never! — would I tell the story which Barak had just told me. Or so I thought at the time.

Epilogue

Twenty-three years have passed since the battle.

Deborah plucks the strings of her lyre. About thirty men stand in the clearing around the palm tree. They wait eagerly, watching as she sits on the bench.

A cool breeze flutters the leaves of the trees. The sun beats warmly upon us as we listen to the shaphat of Israel. In the peace of the Sabbath, she will sing for us, as her custom has been for years. Her song is now the most popular song in all Israel, even more loved and treasured than the famous Song of Miriam.

She wears no head covering, something she would not have had enough self-assurance to do in her youth. Her pure white hair streams down below her shoulders. Her waist is still thin, and she carries herself regally. I recall fondly the shy, meek girl I had brought to this place almost forty years ago. This is the same person, but she has changed.

She sings.

Listen, O you kings,
Pay attention, all rulers.
For I sing about Yahweh,
The God of Israel.

It is now known as Deborah's Song. Of course I composed the words, but nobody knows that. Or cares. They only know it is Deborah's Song. And I will never tell them differently.

She sings about the time many years ago, twenty-three to be exact, when the Canaanites dominated the land. Caravans no longer traveled across Israel, selling their wares. The main roads were deserted, except for those who journeyed with armed escorts or sneaked along back roads. Those were terrible times, and many of us refuse to forget them, nor will we allow the younger generation to forget. That's why she sings this song every Sabbath.

The Song continues. The trumpet was sounded in Israel. Barak and Deborah called forth the people, rich and poor alike, to do battle for their homeland. They came. The brave men responded to the call of their leaders, from the tribes of Ephraim, and Benjamin, and Zebulon, and Manassah. They came to fight for Yahweh.

In my original poem, I had railed against

the tribes which did not come, notably Reuben, Gad, and Asher. But she never sings of that. Others do, however. They will not allow anyone to forget the ones who didn't show up.

As she sings, she strums hard when she comes to the battle scene.

The kings of Canaan fought at Taanach,
By Megiddo's springs, they challenged,
But they won no victory.
The stars in their courses fought against Sisera.
The flood of the Kishon River swept them
   away.

Then comes the climax of the song, the mighty epic of valor which resulted in the death of Sisera.

Blessed be Jael, the wife of Heber the Kenite.
Blessed be Jael, above all women who live in
   tents.
Sisera asked for water, and she gave him milk,
Milk! In a beautiful cup.
Then she took a tent peg in one hand,
A workman's hammer in the other.
She struck Sisera and pierced his temple.
She crushed his head.
She pounded the pin through his skull,
And he lay at her feet . . . dead!

Why is it that the people of Israel never tire of hearing the gory details of this event? Jael has become the great folk-hero of Israel. Deborah herself has insisted on that. I don't know if it is her natural shyness and humility, or if she believes it is the will of Yahweh that Jael, not Deborah, should be the honored woman in Israel. In any case, Deborah's humble pose does her more honor than shame. At least in my opinion.

The closing scene in the song was inspired by Deborah's sensitive mind as she pictured the scene. As sung by Deborah, it never fails to move her audience.

The mother of Sisera watched through the
    window.
She waited and watched for her son to come
    home.
"Why is his chariot so late in coming?
Why don't we hear the sound of his wheels?"
Her ladies-in-waiting answered her,
And she believed, wanting to be comforted,
"There is too much loot to be divided.
It takes too much time.
A girl or two for every soldier,
And gorgeous robes for Sisera,
Which he will bring home to his wife,
To adorn the body of his queen."

Then, according to her custom, she pauses before singing the last lines.

So may all your enemies perish, Yahweh.
But may those who love you rise,
Shining brightly as the sun.

As always, Deborah's Song brings tears to the eyes of the men. Mine, too. I have heard the song over and over again, and it has never failed to move me.

My nephew Modan is here. He stands in the crowd, his gray beard falling on his chest. He gazes adoringly at Deborah.

Modan is my heir. We have no children, Deborah and I. Yahweh has chosen not to honor Deborah that way. I accepted this long ago, although with no small amount of bitterness. But I could not change the will of Yahweh.

Modan's father Rakem has never been avenged. Nor will he. Everyone has forgotten my foolish vow of vengeance.

As everyone will forget me. I shall never be known in the Sacred Story of Israel as Beriah ben Jonathan, proud descendent of Ephraim ben Joseph. Instead I shall always be Eshet Lappidoth, spouse of the spirit-filled woman.

And Deborah shall always be remembered

not only as the shaphat of Israel, but also as its mother. This is the will of Yahweh.

So let it be, forever.